Here·be·Monsters!

BOOK 1

PANTS AHOY!

OXFORD

HERE·BE·MONSTERS!

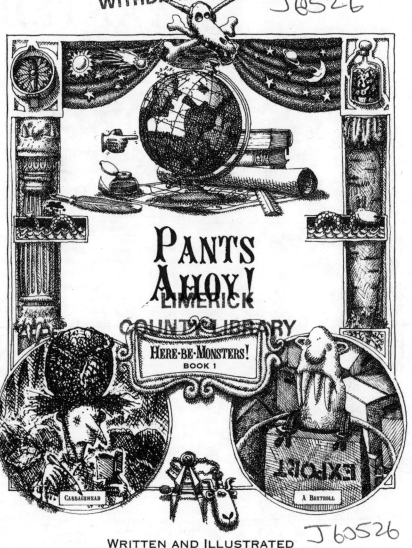

PANTS AHOY!

HERE·BE·MONSTERS!
BOOK 1

CABBAGEHEAD

A BOXTROLL

EXPORT

WRITTEN AND ILLUSTRATED
by Alan Snow

To Edward, and with enormous thanks
to everyone who has helped along the way

OXFORD
UNIVERSITY PRESS

Great Clarendon Street, Oxford OX2 6DP

Oxford University Press is a department of the University of Oxford.
It furthers the University's objective of excellence in research, scholarship,
and education by publishing worldwide in

Oxford   New York

Auckland   Cape Town   Dar es Salaam   Hong Kong   Karachi
Kuala Lumpur   Madrid   Melbourne   Mexico City   Nairobi
New Delhi   Shanghai   Taipei   Toronto

With offices in

Argentina   Austria   Brazil   Chile   Czech Republic   France   Greece
Guatemala   Hungary   Italy   Japan   Poland   Portugal   Singapore
South Korea   Switzerland   Thailand   Turkey   Ukraine   Vietnam

Oxford is a registered trade mark of Oxford University Press
in the UK and in certain other countries

First published 2005 as part of *Here Be Monsters!*
First published in this paperback edition 2008

British Library Cataloguing in Publication Data

Data available

ISBN: 978-0-19-275540-7

1 3 5 7 9 10 8 6 4 2

Printed in Great Britain by Cox & Wyman Ltd, Reading, Berkshire.

HERE·BE·MONSTERS!

BOOK 1

PANTS AHOY!

IN WHICH WE LEARN A LITTLE
ABOUT ARTHUR, BOXTROLLS,
CABBAGEHEADS, AND STRANGE
GOINGS-ON IN RATBRIDGE

Contents

JOHNSON'S TAXONOMY
OF TROLLS AND CREATURES

Aardvark
Aardvarks are invariably the first animals listed in any alphabetical listing of creatures. Beyond this they have few attributes relevant here.

Boxtrolls
A sub-species of the common troll, they are very shy, so live inside a box. These they gather from the backs of large shops. They are somewhat troublesome creatures—as they have a passion for everything mechanical and no understanding of the concept of ownership (they steal anything which is not bolted down, and more often than not, anything which is). It is very dangerous to leave tools lying about where they might find them.

Cabbageheads
Belief has it that cabbageheads live deep underground and are the bees of the underworld. Little else is known at this time, apart from a fondness for brassicas.

Cheese
Wild English Cheeses live in bogs. This is unlike their French cousins who live in caves. They are nervous beasties, that eat grass by night, in the meadows and woodlands. They are also of very low intelligence, and are panicked by almost anything that catches them unawares. Cheeses make easy quarry for hunters, being rather easier to catch than a dead sheep.

Crow
The crow is a very intelligent bird, capable of living in many environments. Crows are known to be considerably more honest than their cousins, magpies, and enjoy a varied diet, and good company. Usually they are charming company, but should be kept from providing the entertainment. Failure to do so may result in tedium, for while intelligent, crows seem to lack taste in the choice of music, and conversational topics.

Fresh-water Sea-cow
Distant relative of the manitou. This creature inhabits the canals, and drains of certain West Country towns. A passive creature of large size, and vegetarian habits. They are very kind to their young, and make good mothers.

Grandfather (William)

Arthur's guardian and carer. Grandfather has lived underground for many years in a cave home where he pursues his interests in engineering. All the years in a damp cave have taken their toll, and he now suffers from very bad rheumatism, and a somewhat short temper.

The Man in the Iron Socks

A mysterious shadowy figure said to be much feared by the members of the now defunct Cheese Guild. He is thought to hold a dark secret as well as a large 'Walloper'. His Walloper is the major cause of fear, but he also has a sharp tongue, and a caustic line in wit. History does not relate the reasoning behind his wearing of iron socks.

The Members

Members of the secretive Ratbridge Cheese Guild, that was thought to have died out after the 'Great Cheese Crash'. It was an evil organization that rigged the cheese market, and doctored and adulterated lactose-based food stuffs.

Rabbits

Furry, jumping mammals, with a passion for tender vegetables and raising the young. Good parents, but not very bright.

Rabbit Women

Very little is known about these mythical creatures, except that they are supposed to live with rabbits, and wear clothes spun from rabbit wool.

Rats

Rats are known to be some of the most intelligent of all rodents, and to be considerably more intelligent than many humans. They are known to have a passion for travel, and be extremely adaptable. They often live in a symbiotic relationship with humans.

Trotting Badgers

Trotting badgers are some of the nastiest creatures to be found anywhere. With their foul temper, rapid speed, and razor-sharp teeth, it cannot be stressed just how unpleasant and dangerous these creatures are. It is only their disgusting stench that gives warning of their proximity, and when smelt it is often too late.

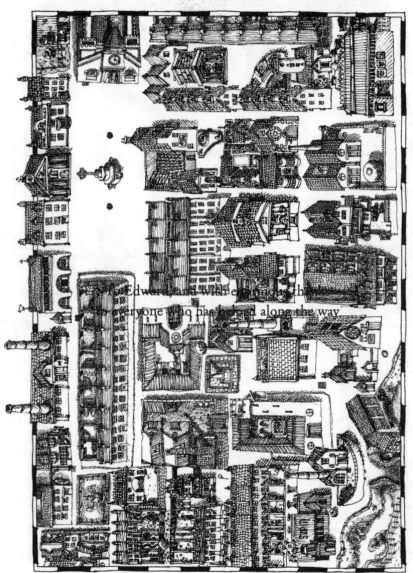

Ratbridge Town Centre

Ratbridge

Chapter 1

COMING UP!

It was a late Sunday evening and Ratbridge stood silver grey and silent in the moonlight. Early evening rain had washed away the cloud of smoke that normally hung over the town, and now long shadows from the factory chimneys fell across oily puddles in the empty streets. The town was at rest.

The shadows moved slowly across the lane that ran behind Fore Street revealing a heavy iron drain cover set amongst the cobbles.

Then the drain cover moved. Something was pushing it up from below.

One side of the cover lifted a few inches, and from beneath it, a pair of eyes scanned the lane. The drain cover lifted further, then slid sideways. A boy's head wearing a woven helmet with nine or ten antennae rose through the hole and glanced around. The boy shut his eyes, and he

A pair of eyes scanned the lane

listened. For a moment all was quiet, then a distant dog bark echoed off the walls. Silence returned. The boy opened his eyes, reached out of the hole, and pulled himself up and out into the lane. He was dressed very strangely. In addition to the helmet he wore a large vest knitted from soft rope, that reached the ground, and under that a short one-piece suit made from old sugar sacks. His feet were wrapped in layers of rough cloth, tied with string.

Fixed about his body by wide leather straps was a strange contraption. On his front was a wooden box with a winding handle on one side, and two brass buttons and a knob on the front. A flexible metal tube connected the box to a pair of folded wings, made from leather, wood, and brass, that were attached to his back.

The boy slid the drain cover back into place, reached inside his under-suit and pulled out a toy figure dressed just like him. He held the doll out and spoke.

'Grandfather, I am up top. I think I'll have to go gardening tonight. It's a Sunday, and everything is shut. The bins behind the inn will be empty.' He looked at the doll.

There was a crackle of static, and a thin voice came from the doll. 'Well, you be careful, Arthur! And remember, only take from the bigger gardens . . . and only then if they have plenty! There are a lot of people that can only survive by growing their own food.'

Arthur smiled. He had heard this many times before. 'Don't worry, Grandfather, I haven't forgotten! I'll only take what we need . . . and I will be careful. I'll see you as soon as I am done.'

'Grandfather, I am up top'

Arthur replaced the doll inside his suit, then started to wind the handle on the box on his front. As he wound it made a soft whirring noise. For nearly two minutes he wound, pausing occasionally when his hand started aching. Then a bell pinged from somewhere inside the box and he stopped. Arthur scanned the skyline, crouched, and then pressed one of the buttons. The wings on his back unfolded. He pressed the other button and at the same moment jumped as high as he could. Silently the wings rushed down and caught the air as he rose. At the bottom of their stroke they folded, rose, and then beat down again. His wings were holding him in the air, a few feet above the ground. Arthur's hand reached for the knob and he turned it just a little. As he did so he tilted himself a little forward. He started to move. Arthur smiled . . . he was flying.

He was flying

He moved slowly down the lane, keeping below the top of its walls. When he reached the end, he adjusted the knob again, and rose up to a gap between the twin roofs of the Glue Factory. Arthur knew routes that were safe from the eyes of the townsfolk, and would keep to one of these tonight on the way to the particular garden he planned on visiting. When it was dark or there was thick smog, things were easy. But tonight was clear and the moon full. He'd been spotted twice before on nights like these, by children, from their bedroom windows. He'd got away with it so far, as nobody had believed them when they said they had seen a fairy or flying boy, but tonight he was not going to take any chances.

He adjusted the knob

A horse started and whinnied as he flew over

Arthur reached the end of the gap between the roofs. He dipped a little and flew across a large stable yard. A horse started and whinnied as he flew over. He adjusted his wing speed and increased his height. The horse made him feel uneasy. At the far side of the yard he rose again over a huge gate, topped with spikes. He crossed a deserted alley, then moved down a narrow street flanked with the windowless backs of houses. At the far end of the street he slowed and then hovered in the air. In front of him was another high wall. Carefully he adjusted the knob, and rose very gently to the point where he could just see the ground beyond the wall. It was a large vegetable garden. Across the garden fell paths of pale light, cast from the windows of the house. Arthur looked towards it. One of the windows was open. From it he could hear raised voices and the clatter of dominoes.

That should keep them busy! he thought, scanning the garden again. Against the wall furthest from the house was a large glass lean-to.

He checked the windows of the house again, then rose over the wall and headed for the greenhouse, keeping above the beams of light from the house. He came to rest in front of the greenhouse door.

Silently Arthur turned off and folded his wings. He opened the door, and a soft rush of warm perfumed air brushed his face. It was a mixture of smells—some familiar, some not.

Dark leafy forms filled the greenhouse. Some were suspended from the roof, while others climbed almost invisible strings. Some larger ones just hogged the ground. As Arthur entered he recognized tomato plants climbing the strings, and cucumbers and grapes hanging from above.

He moved past all these, and made his way to a tree against the far wall.

It was a tall tree with branches only at its top. Dangling from a stem below the branches was what looked like a stack of huge fat upside-down spiders. It was a large bunch of bananas. As Arthur got closer he caught their scent. It was beautiful.

Arthur could hardly contain his delight. Bananas! He tore one from the bunch, then peeled and ate it ravenously. When he had finished it, he turned and checked the house. Nothing had changed. Turning back to the tree, he reached inside his under-suit and pulled out a string bag, then reached up to the banana bunch and pulled eagerly. It was

What looked like a huge stack of fat upside-down spiders

not as easy to pick the full bunch as it had been to pull off a single banana, and Arthur found he had to put his full weight on the bunch. A soft fibrous tearing sound started, but still the bunch did not come down. In desperation, Arthur lifted his feet from the ground and swung his legs. All of a sudden there was a crack and the whole bunch, along with Arthur, fell to the ground. The tree trunk sprang back up and struck the glass roof with a loud crack. The noise sounded out across the garden.

'Oi! There is something in the greenhouse,' came a shout from the house.

Hearing the shout, Arthur scrambled to his feet, grabbed the string bag and looked out through the glass. No one was in the garden yet. He rushed to collect up as many of the bananas as possible, shoving them into the bag. Then he heard a door bang and the sound of footsteps. He ran out of the greenhouse into the garden.

A very large lady with a very long stick

Clambering towards him over the rows of vegetables was a very large lady with a very long stick. Arthur dashed over to one of the garden walls, stabbed at the buttons on the front of his box, and jumped. His wings snapped open and started to beat, but not strongly enough to lift him. He landed back on the ground, his wings fluttering behind him. Arthur groaned—the bananas! He had to adjust the wings for the extra weight. But he was not ready to put the bananas down and fly away empty-handed—they were too precious. Still clutching the string bag with the bananas in one hand, he grabbed for the knob on the front of the box with the other hand, and twisted it hard. The wings immediately doubled their beating and became a blur. Just as the woman reached the spot where Arthur stood, he shot almost vertically upwards, just avoiding her outstretched hand. Furious, she swung her stick above her head and, before he could get out of range, landed a hard blow on his wings, sending him spinning.

'You little varmint! Come down here and give me back my bananas!' the woman cried. Arthur grasped at the top of the wall to steady himself. The stick now swished inches below his feet. He adjusted the wings quickly, and made off over the wall. Shouts of anger followed him. J60526 .

Arthur felt sick to the pit of his stomach. Coming up at night to collect food was always risky, and this was the closest he'd ever been to being caught. He needed somewhere quiet to rest and recover.

I wish we could live above ground like everybody else! he thought.

Now he flew across the town by the safest route he knew—flying between roofs, up the darkest alleys, and across deserted yards, till finally he reached the abandoned Cheese Hall. He knew he would be alone here.

The Cheese Hall had been the grandest of all the buildings in the town and was only overshadowed by a few of the factory chimneys. In former times, it had been the home of the Ratbridge Cheese Guild. But now the industry was dead, and the Guild and all its members ruined. The Hall was now boarded up and deserted. Its gilded statues that once shone out across the town were blackened by the very soot that had poisoned the cheese.

The Cheese Hall

Arthur landed on the bridge of the roof, and settled himself amongst the statues. As he sat catching his breath it occurred to him that maybe he should inspect his wings for damage. The woman had landed a fairly heavy blow, but Arthur decided it would be too dangerous and awkward to take his wings off high up here on the roof, and besides they seemed to be fine. Something distracted him from his thoughts—a noise. It sounded like a mournful bleat, from somewhere below. He listened carefully, intrigued, but heard no more. When he finally felt calm again, he stowed the bananas behind one of the statues, climbed out from his hiding place, and flew up to the best observation spot in the whole town. This was the plinth on the top of the dome that supported the weathervane and lightning conductor.

A complete panorama of the town and the surrounding countryside, broken only by the chimneystacks of the factories, was laid out before him. In the far distance he could just make out some sort of procession in the moonlight making for the woods. It looked as though something was being chased by a group of horses.

The plinth that supported the weathervane and lightning conductor

North East Bumbleshire

Three large barrel cheeses broke from the undergrowth

Chapter 2

THE HUNT

Strange sounds were filtering through the woods—scrabblings, bleatings and growlings—and, strangest of all, a sound closely resembling bagpipes, or the sound bagpipes would make if they were being strangled, viciously, under a blanket. In a small moonlit clearing in the centre of the woods the sounds grew louder. Suddenly there was a frantic rustling in the bushes on one side of the clearing, and three large barrel cheeses broke from the undergrowth, running as fast as their legs would carry them. Hurtling across the clearing, bleating in panic, they disappeared into the bushes on the far side of the clearing, and for a moment all was still again.

Suddenly a new burst of rustling came from the bushes where the cheeses had emerged, along with a horrid growling noise. Then a pack of hounds burst out into the open. They were a motley bunch, all different shapes and sizes, but they all had muzzles covering their snouts, and they all shared the awful reek of sweat. The hounds ran around in circles, growling through their muzzles. One small fat animal that looked like a cross between a sausage dog and a ball of wire wool kept his nose to the ground, sniffing intently. He gave a great snort, crossed the clearing, and dived onwards after the cheeses. The other hounds followed.

They were a motley bunch, all different shapes and sizes

The weird bagpipe sound grew closer, accompanied by vaguely human cries. Then there was a louder crashing in the undergrowth and finally the strangest creature yet arrived in the clearing. It had four skinny legs that hung from what looked like an upturned boat made from a patchwork of old sacking. At its front was a head made from an old box, and on this the features of a horse's face were crudely drawn. A large angry man rode high on its back.

'Which way did they go?' the man screamed.

An arm emerged from the sacking and pointed across the clearing. The rider took his horn (made from some part of a camel), and blew, filling the clearing with the horrible

A large angry man rode high on its back

bagpipe-like sound. Then he raised the horn high in the air and brought it down hard on his steed.

'Hummgggiff Gummmminn Hoofff!' came muffled cries of pain from below.

The creature started to move in a wobbly line across the clearing, picking up speed as the rider beat it harder. More men on these strange creatures arrived in the clearing, following the sound of the horn. They were just in time to catch the lead rider disappearing. They too beat their mounts. As they did, shouts of 'Tally-ho!' and 'Gee-up!' could be heard over the cries from the beasts below.

The front legs of the last of these creatures came to a sudden halt. However, the back legs kept moving and, inevitably, caught up with the front legs. There was an Ooof! and a sweaty red face emerged from the front of the creature. The head looked up at the rider and spoke.

'That's it, Trout! I have had enough! I want a go on top.'

'But I only got a "turn" since the start of the woods, and

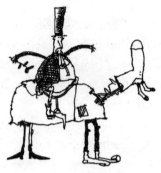

A sweaty red face emerged from the front of the creature

you had a long go across the fields,' moaned the rider. Another face now emerged from the back end of the creature, and joined in.

'Yes! . . . and Gristle, you tried to make us jump that gate!'

'Well, I'm not going on, and I'll blame you two if we get in trouble for getting left behind,' said the face at the front.

'All right then!' the rider said with a pout.

He jumped down, and as he took off his jacket and top hat, the creature's body lifted to reveal two men underneath. The

The creature's body lifted to reveal two men underneath

man at the front unstrapped himself, and the rider took his place. The body lowered itself and the new rider put on the jacket and hat, and climbed with some difficulty into the saddle.

'Don't you dare try going through the stream,' the back end of the creature demanded.

'All right, but make sure we catch up,' said the new rider. 'You know the rules about being last!'

He then grabbed a large twig from an overhanging branch, snapped it off, and belted the back end of his mount. With a short scream and some cursing, the creature set off. Quiet returned to the clearing.

The woods now disgorged a weird procession. First the cheeses, then after a few moments the hounds, followed by the huntsmen. Baying filled the night air as the hounds got a clear sight of their quarry. Fear drove the cheeses faster. The hounds gained on them and as they did the cheeses' bleating became ever more mournful . . .

With a short scream and some cursing, the creature set off

A weird procession

Then the first of the cheese-hounds struck. One of the smaller cheeses was trailing a few yards behind the rest. It was an easy target. In one leap, the hound landed its front paws on the cheese. Whimpering and bleating, the cheese struggled to get free, but it was no good. Its legs buckled, and it collapsed on the grass. The dog rolled the cheese onto its side with its snout, and held it down firmly with his paws. Most of the other hounds raced after the other fleeing cheeses, but a few dogs paused long enough to worry the trapped cheese, growling threateningly. As they did so the leader of the hunt laboured up on his mount and clonked them mercilessly with his horn.

Then the first of the cheese-hounds struck

'Back to the chase, you lazy dairy-pugs!' he yelled. 'Gherkin! Deal with this 'ere cheese!'

'Yes, Master!' replied a stubby rider close behind. He slowed his mount, stopped close to the cheese, and climbed down. Throwing a piece of dried bread to the ground to distract the hound, Gherkin put a boot on the cheese to keep it pinned down, then took some string from his pocket and

Gherkin dealing with the cheese

tied it firmly to the cheese's ankle. Keeping a tight hold on the string, Gherkin climbed back on to his mount.

'Right, my boys, it's a gentle ride home for us,' said Gherkin, stirring his mount back towards the town.

'It might be a gentle ride home for you, Gherkin, but it's a damnable long walk for us!' a muffled voice grunted from under the saddle. Still, off they set with the cheese in tow. The hunt was now in the distance, picking off the rest of the cheeses. Their mournful cries were being replaced by a resigned silence.

Off they set with the cheese in tow

The Cheese Hall

He grabbed his doll from under his suit

Chapter 3

FROM ON HIGH

Arthur watched it all from his perch on top of the Cheese Hall. The procession drew closer to Ratbridge and now he could make out most of the creatures involved. It slowly dawned on him what was happening. It was a cheese hunt!

He grabbed his doll from under his suit, and raised it to his mouth.

'Grandfather! Grandfather! It's Arthur. Can you hear me?' There was a crackling and his grandfather replied.

'Yes, Arthur, I can hear you. What's happening?'

'I think I can see a cheese hunt!'

There was a pause, then Grandfather spoke again. 'Are you sure? Cheese hunting is illegal. Where are you?'

'I am sitting on top of the Cheese Hall. I am . . .' Arthur decided to gloss over earlier events. '. . . having a break. I can see the whole thing. Riders and hounds chasing and catching cheeses.'

'But they can't! It's cruel, and illegal!' Grandfather sputtered. 'Are you sure there are riders on horses?'

'Yes, Grandfather. Why?'

'Because all the cheese hunting horses were sold off to the Glue Factory after the great Cheese Crash.'

'Well, they do seem to be riding horses . . . but there's something rather odd about them,' Arthur told him.

'They do seem to be riding horses'

'What is it?'

'They're very ungainly, and somewhat oddly shaped . . . I can see that even from here. Who do you think is doing the hunting?'

'I am not sure,' said Grandfather. 'Where are they now?'

'They are approaching the West Gate.'

'Well, they must be from the town then. If we could find out who was responsible, perhaps we could do something to put a stop to it. Do you think you could have a closer look without being seen?'

'Yes, I think so,' Arthur said, starting to feel excited.

'Well, keep up on the roofs, and see if you can follow them.' Grandfather paused. 'BUT . . . be very careful!'

'Don't worry, I will be.'

'And call me if you find out anything.'

'All right. I'll speak to you later. And, Grandfather . . . I've got some bananas.'

'Err . . . Well . . . err . . . I rather like bananas . . .' Grandfather's voice trailed off.

Arthur put the doll away and wound his wings again. Here at last was a chance for some real adventure.

Here at last was a chance for some real adventure

Cheese hunting is illegal!

He pulled out a large black iron key

Chapter 4

INTO THE TOWN

By the time the hunt reached the West Gate, they had nine cheeses in tow. The hounds were exhausted. As the chase was over, their muzzles had been removed. Snatcher, the leader of the hunt, manoeuvred his mount till he was within arm's length of the thick wooden gate. He pulled a large black iron key out of his topcoat, leaned over and unlocked it. Gristle, on the horse behind him, dismounted and swung the gate open.

Arthur flew from the Cheese Hall to a rooftop near the gate, and settled out of sight behind a parapet. He looked down.

In the street below the hunt wove its way into town. It was a terrifying sight. Strange four-legged creatures were carrying very ugly men in very tall hats. A pack of manky hounds sniffed around behind them, and just visible in the

He looked down

shadows were short tubby yellow cheeses tied with pieces of string to some of the riders. One of these cheeses stumbled on the cobbles and let out a bleat.

'Quick!' hissed Snatcher. 'Muffle 'im! We don't want to get caught.'

One of the riders threw a large sack over the cheese and it fell silent. The rider scooped up the sack and the procession continued on its way.

Arthur moved along the parapet till he reached the end of the building. An alley divided him from the next house. He

The procession continued on its way

pressed the buttons on the front of his box, rose silently and flew towards the next house. He was proud of himself—he had not made a single sound that had attracted their attention. But what he had not accounted for was the position of the moon. As he crossed the alley his shadow fell across the street.

Cheeses have many predators, but the one that they fear most is the Cheese Hawk. The merest hint of anything large and flapping will send cheeses into a blind panic. Arthur's flapping shadow was too much for them. All hell broke loose.

Arthur's flapping shadow was too much for them

One cheese let out a sharp cry. This set off the other cheeses. The riders were caught off guard, and had the strings ripped from their hands as the cheeses bolted . . . straight under the legs of the 'mounts'. Two of the mounts tripped over the cheeses and collapsed, throwing their riders to the ground. The riders following them were unable to halt their mounts and they too all piled into the heap. The hounds now went crazy. In their excited state, with no muzzles to hold them back, they set upon all the available human limbs sticking out of the heap. This caused much screaming and wailing. In the middle of the confusion, only Snatcher and his mount were left standing. He looked up and caught Arthur in his stare.

They all piled into a heap

'What do we have 'ere?' he said to himself with a mixture of malice and curiosity.

Arthur watched the commotion in shock. He twisted round to get a better look and in the moment of doing so, it became clear that the blow from the banana woman's stick had damaged his wings.

There was a snapping sound and he felt himself jerk to one side . . . then start to drop. He was falling! Arthur grabbed for the knob and twisted it hard. Still he dropped. His broken right wing was just dragging limply above him like a streamer. Snatcher was driving his mount towards the ground below him. In a last desperate attempt, Arthur reached for the handle on the side of the box and started to wind for all he was worth. The remaining wing sped up. Harder and harder he wound. His descent slowed to a stop . . . just above Snatcher.

Just above Snatcher

Still Arthur wound, harder and harder. Then he felt something grab his ankle. Arthur tried to pull away. There was a cackling from below.

''Ow ingenious! I always rather fancied flying,' came a voice.

'Let me go!' cried Arthur.

'I shall not!' came the reply, and Arthur felt a sharp tug, swinging him around, and the tip of his broken wing poked Snatcher straight in the left eye.

'Wwwaaaahhhh!'

'Wwwwwwwwwwwaaaaaaaaaaaaaaaaaaahhhh!!' Snatcher cried,

releasing his grip on Arthur's ankle and putting a hand to his eye. As soon as he was released Arthur rose a little. Still winding he kicked off from one of the walls and started down the alley. Behind him he could hear a very pained Snatcher.

'Faster, faster, get the little tyke!' screamed Snatcher.

Though he kept winding, there was no way Arthur could get high enough to escape over the roofs—his damaged wing could barely keep him above the ground. To get back to the drain, he would have to make his way through the streets and alleys, he thought wildly. But the cheese-hounds were now snapping below him, and he wound faster still, trying to keep above their reach . . .

Snapping below

Ahead of him the alley faded into darkness, and he turned through an archway into a yard beyond. With a start of relief, Arthur realized he knew where he was. The yard backed onto the lane where the drain—and the way home—was. He had a chance of getting there, if his wings would just hold out long enough. The wall dividing him from the lane was only a few feet higher than he was flying. He might just make it. The barking grew louder again. Arthur wound and adjusted the knob at the same time, twisting it with all his might and willing himself over the wall.

But the remaining wing could not take any more. With a sharp tearing noise, the leather tore away from the wing spars. Arthur frantically reached out for the wall, but it was no good. He was falling—and the cheese-hounds were waiting for him below. Dropping to the ground, he spun round to face the drooling hounds, bracing himself for the worst. There was no way he could fight them off. But they held back, seeming to be a little scared by the flailing wing spar.

He faced the drooling hounds

For a wild moment Arthur wondered if he could somehow beat them back, but then there was a crunching noise from the box and the skeleton of the last wing stopped. The hounds started to spread out in a circle around him. They were growling and snapping, looking for a chance to pounce. Desperately, Arthur tore one of the wing spars from his back, and spun around to confront any dog that seemed to be getting closer. Every time he did, the hounds on the other side would start to creep forward. He noticed a water butt in the corner of the yard, next to the back wall. Perhaps if he could manage to get onto that, he might have a chance. Fending off the dogs, he moved towards the butt. The hounds moved with him. Then Arthur's heart sank again. Snatcher entered the yard. He quickly dismounted and walked towards Arthur, holding a hand over his injured eye.

'No you don't, you little vermin. I have plans for you! . . . And your wings,' he wheezed.

'No you don't, you little vermin'

The man's eye now was so swollen that it had closed.

'It's just as well that you poked me in me glass eye,' Snatcher hissed, 'or I'd have had to come up with something even more unpleasant than I've got planned for you!'

Snatcher snarled and made a lunge for Arthur. Arthur jumped back, and bumped into the butt. He was completely cornered.

'Now, boy, give me those wings of yours. I am very interested in contraptions! Take 'em off now! Now!' Snatcher ordered.

Arthur slowly reached for the buckle on one of his shoulders.

'Faster, boy!' Snatcher snapped. 'Get 'em off quick, or I'll be setting the hounds on yer!'

Arthur released one buckle, then another and finally the last one at his side. The wings were now loose.

Snatcher grabbed the wings

'Give 'em 'ere!' Snatcher hissed.

Arthur slipped the wings over his head, and as he did so Snatcher grabbed them.

'Clever, very clever . . . might well be useful!' Snatcher mused as he turned the remains of the wings over in his huge hands.

Arthur stood with his back against the water butt, glancing from the snapping dogs to Snatcher. Grandfather had warned him so many times about being careful. Now, having made just one mistake, he was in real trouble for the first time in his life. The dogs took their chance and moved closer as Snatcher's attention was not on them.

Then one of the larger hounds made a lunge for him. Arthur kicked out just in time and caught the dog's nose with his toe. The dog pulled back with a whimper, and Snatcher looked up.

Arthur kicked out just in time

'You just keep him there, me pugs.' He smirked, and turned back to his inspection.

Arthur slowly moved his hands back onto the butt then, stealthily, always keeping an eye on Snatcher, he pulled himself up till he was sitting on the edge of it. The hounds started to growl and strain forward, but Snatcher was so absorbed in the wings that he absent-mindedly shushed them. So, careful not to make a sound, Arthur raised his knees till his heels were resting on the edge of the butt.

The hounds started to growl and strain forward

He glanced up at the top of the wall, and one of the hounds let out a bark. Snatcher looked up and realized what was happening. He let out a cry of rage just as Arthur jumped up, turned, grabbed the top of the wall and pulled himself over it.

He fell flat to the ground on the other side, and winded himself. He lay for a few seconds trying to catch his breath, and listened to the shouts of anger and barking from over the wall.

'Get round the back and 'ave im! You mutts!' Snatcher bellowed. There was the sound of leather on dog and then a loud howling.

He fell flat to the ground

Arthur scrambled to his feet and started for the drain cover at the far end of the lane. Then he heard the hounds coming round the corner. He wasn't going to make it. He ducked into a doorway in the wall, then peeped back out. Snatcher, surrounded by hounds, stood right by the drain cover. There were more footsteps and the rest of the riders appeared.

Snatcher, surrounded by hounds, stood by the drain cover

'I think he went down here! Must live down below! Go and get the glue and an iron plate!' Snatcher ordered. A group of the hunters disappeared.

Snatcher turned and scanned the alley. 'OK, the rest of you search the alley, just in case.'

The men stood for a moment while hounds sniffed the air. Then the little dog that looked like a cross between a sausage dog and a ball of wire wool started to make his way down the alley directly towards Arthur. Arthur pressed his back against the door. This time there really was no way out. A shiver of fear went through him at the thought of what Snatcher would do to him when he got hold of him. Suddenly he felt the door give way behind him. Something grabbed him around the knees, pulled him through the doorway, and the door slammed shut.

Arthur pressed his back against the door

The shop

It framed a boxtroll

Chapter 5

HERE BE MONSTERS!

Arthur found himself standing in total darkness. The overwhelming relief at having got away from Snatcher and his hounds was mixed with the awful fear that he might have been dragged into something even worse. Who or what had pulled him through that door and why? A soft gurgling noise came from somewhere behind him. He turned round towards it, and trod on something. There was a squeak, a scuffling of feet, and the sound of a doorknob being turned. Light broke in as a door opened. It framed a boxtroll, its smiling head protruding from its large cardboard box.

Arthur had seen boxtrolls before, underground. He would occasionally come across them as he explored the dark passages, caverns, and tunnels. Boxtrolls were timid creatures and always scuttled away as soon as they noticed his presence. This was the first time Arthur had seen one close at hand, and it now stood smiling, and beckoning to him.

Arthur walked towards it hesitantly. The boxtroll turned and scampered up a huge heap of nuts and bolts that covered the floor of the room ahead. As it reached the top, it stopped and picked up a handful of the nuts and bolts. Arthur stared as it lifted them to its mouth and kissed them. It then sprinkled them back over the heap, and grinned at him. Arthur had heard that boxtrolls loved everything mechanical, and he'd seen their work everywhere underground, draining the passages, and shoring up the tunnels and caves.

Beckoning to Arthur again, the boxtroll turned and scuttled out of the doorway on the other side of the room. Arthur clambered over the heap and followed it into a small hallway. Ahead of them was a panelled door. The top panels were made of glass, and through them a warm yellow light shone. The boxtroll knocked on the door.

'Come on in, Fish!' a muffled voice replied.

The boxtroll turned again to Arthur and smiled. Then it opened the door, walked a few steps into the room, and cleared its throat.

'Well, what is it, Fish? What treasures have you brought to show us this evening?' A man's voice came from somewhere inside the room. 'Come on then, let's have a look!'

The boxtroll reached back. It took Arthur's hand and led him into the room.

Arthur's jaw fell open. From amongst the cages, tanks,

The boxtroll turned again to Arthur and smiled

boxes, old sofas, clocks, brass bedstead, piles of straw, heaps of books, and who knew what else, stared four pairs of eyes. There were two more boxtrolls sitting on a shelf, a small man with a cabbage tied to the top of his head, and an old man. The old man sat in a huge high-backed leather armchair. He was wearing half glasses and a grey wig, and was smiling at Arthur.

'Hello. Who do we have here?' the old man enquired in a gentle voice.

Arthur blinked. The old man waited patiently.

'I'm Arthur!' he finally said.

'Well, Arthur, are you a friend of Fish?' the old man asked.

The old man sat in a huge high-backed leather armchair

Two other boxtrolls made spluttering noises. The boxtroll holding Arthur's hand turned to him, squeezed his hand, and made a happy gurgling sound.

'Yes,' said the old man, 'I think you are!' He looked sternly at the two boxtrolls on the shelf. 'And Shoe and Egg should know better than to snigger at Fish!' The two boxtrolls fell silent, their faces turning bright red.

Arthur looked around the room. It was packed to overflowing. If you took a junk shop, added the contents of a small zoo, then threw all your household possessions on

The two boxtrolls fell silent, their faces turning bright red

top, it would start to give you an idea of what it was like. It smelt a little of compost. But it was warm and quiet, everyone looked friendly—and, best of all, there were no hounds snapping at him.

He had no idea where he was, but he did know that he felt safe. Safe enough to ask a question himself.

'Please, sir, may I ask you who you are?' asked Arthur.

'Certainly, young man!' the old man grinned. 'I am Willbury Nibble QC . . . Retired! I was a lawyer, but now I live here with my companions.'

Arthur looked about. 'What is this place?'

'Oh, this place was a pet shop, but now I rent it to live in. And these are my friends,' Willbury said, looking around at the creatures. 'You have met Fish already it would seem, and these two reprobates,' he nodded at the other boxtrolls, 'are Shoe and Egg.'

The boxtrolls on the shelf smiled at Arthur. Then the old man turned to the last creature—the little man with the cabbage on his head. 'And this is Titus. He is a cabbagehead.'

The cabbagehead scurried behind the old man's chair.

'I am afraid he is rather nervous. He'll get used to you, though, and then you will find him charming.'

'I am afraid he is rather nervous'

A cabbagehead! Grandfather had told Arthur stories about cabbageheads. Legend had it that they lived in the caverns deep underground. It was said that they grew strange vegetables there, and worshipped cabbages. This had something to do with why they tied cabbages to their heads. Even Grandfather had not seen a cabbagehead, they were so shy.

Arthur thought to himself for a moment then asked, 'Your friends are all underlings, so why do they live with you?'

Willbury smiled with bemusement. 'What do you know about underlings, Arthur?'

'I know that the boxtrolls look after the tunnels and plumbing underground. But I don't know much about cabbageheads,' said Arthur.

They lived in the caverns deep underground

'Well, I am not sure I entirely approve, but our boxtroll friends here act as scouts.' Willbury gave the boxtrolls a funny look.

'Scouts?' asked Arthur.

'Yes. It would seem that the boxtrolls have a need for certain supplies to help with their maintenance of the Underworld. So Fish, Shoe, and Egg wander the town looking for . . . "supplies"! When they find them they "prepare" the item for removal—loosen it, unbolt it, unscrew it, whatever. That's why there is such a large heap of nuts and bolts in the back room. God help me if I was ever visited by the police.'

'They "prepare" the item for removal'

He looked rather severely at the boxtrolls, then resumed speaking. 'They leave signs for the other boxtrolls. You may have seen strange chalk marks on the walls about town. These are there to guide the other boxtrolls to the "supplies" so they can make a quick getaway!'

A quick getaway

Arthur looked across at Fish, who grinned and nodded.

'Yes,' said Willbury, rather sternly. 'I don't think I approve at all. Our friends the boxtrolls have a rather strange attitude towards ownership. Have you not noticed that most of your arrows point at someone else's property?'

The boxtrolls looked rather guilty. Arthur felt a little guilty himself remembering the bananas he had left on top of the Cheese Hall.

With all this talk of 'supplies' Arthur thought it was time to change the subject. 'And your friend Titus?'

Willbury beamed. 'He is researching gardening. The cabbageheads are always trying to improve their methods of cultivation. So occasionally one of them spends some time up here studying human gardening methods. Titus has been here a few weeks. Egg and Shoe discovered him one night sleeping in a coalbunker and brought him back. He's been here for a few weeks writing up a report on gardening. When he's finished he will go back to the Underworld.'

Willbury looked behind his chair and said coaxingly, 'Titus, I think our new friend might like to see your report if you would like to show it to him.'

The cabbagehead shot from behind Willbury's chair to a barrel that stood in one corner of the shop. There was a hole cut in its side just big enough for Titus to clamber through. He disappeared and re-emerged carrying something. He ran back and hid behind the chair. A hand offering a small green notebook appeared.

The pages were covered with tiny writing and drawings

Willbury took the notebook and opened it. Arthur leaned over to look. The pages were covered with tiny writing and the most beautiful drawings of plants.

A squeak came from behind the chair. Willbury closed the notebook, winked at Arthur, and passed it over his shoulder to an outstretched hand. The notebook disappeared.

'Now, Arthur, please sit down, if you wish.' Willbury lifted his feet from a footstool, and pushed it towards Arthur. Arthur sat.

'So what brings you here?' asked Willbury.

Arthur suddenly felt overwhelmed. He didn't know where to begin. Fish came forward, and started talking.

Arthur suddenly felt overwhelmed

'Hummif gommmong shoegger tooff!!!'

'I think it would be better if Arthur explained what's happened himself, Fish,' said Willbury. He smiled encouragingly at Arthur. 'Are you in trouble?' asked Willbury.

'Yes,' whispered Arthur. There was a pause.

'Well, let's hear what kind of trouble it is. We'll try to help you if we can. I have spent my whole life trying to sort out trouble for other people,' said Willbury.

Arthur hesitated, then decided he could trust Willbury. 'Yes, I am in trouble. I live underground with Grandfather . . . and now they've blocked my hole back. It's the only way I know to get home . . . And they have taken my wings!' Speaking the words aloud made Arthur realize fully what a terrible situation he was in. Would he ever be able to get back to Grandfather?

'All right,' said Willbury, looking concerned. 'I think you had better tell me the full story.'

Arthur started. 'I'm from the Underworld . . . well, I have lived there since I was a baby.'

Willbury looked curious. 'You live underground?'

'Yes . . . Me and my grandfather live in a cave . . . well, three caves actually. One we use as a living room and kitchen, another is Grandfather's bedroom and workshop, and the smallest is mine. It's my bedroom.' Arthur looked around the shop. 'It's warm and cosy, a bit like this place.'

'Well, three caves actually'

'But why do you live underground?' Willbury asked in a puzzled voice.

Arthur paused for a few moments. 'I'm . . . I'm not really sure. Grandfather always tells me he'll explain when I'm older.'

'And what about your parents?'

Arthur looked sad. 'I don't know . . . I am a "foundling" I think.'

'But your grandfather?'

'Oh . . . He's not my real grandfather, he just found me abandoned on the steps of the workhouse, when I was a baby, and took me back to live with him. He's raised me like he was my father, but because he's so much older than my father would be I call him "Grandfather".'

'So has he always lived underground?'

Arthur thought for a moment. 'No, he said he lived in the town when he was younger . . . But he doesn't talk about it . . . ' Arthur's voice trailed off.

Willbury decided to change the subject a little. 'You say "they" have blocked your hole back to the underground and taken your wings? Who is "they"?'

Arthur spoke mournfully. 'I saw these men hunting cheese and I went to have a look, but my wings broke and the hunters took them and then I escaped, and was trying to get back down underground when they blocked up my hole.'

'But what were you doing above ground? And what wings? I don't understand,' said Willbury.

Arthur decided to tell Willbury all. His face grew red. 'I was gathering food. It's the only way we can survive. My grandfather is so frail now that I have to do it. And he made me some wings so I could get about the town easily.'

'Your grandfather made you wings?'

'Yes, he can make anything. He made my doll as well so I could talk to him while I am above ground.' Arthur reached inside his under-suit and pulled out the doll to show Willbury.

Willbury's eyes grew wide. 'Do you mean to say that you can talk with your grandfather, using this doll?'

'Yes,' said Arthur.

'Does it still work?' asked Willbury.

Arthur looked at the doll closely

'Yes . . . I think so.' Arthur looked at the doll closely—it didn't look damaged in any way.

'When did you last speak to your grandfather?'

'An hour or so ago when I was sitting on top of the Cheese Hall.'

'On top of—oh, never mind. Does he know what's happened to you or where you are?'

'No . . .' said Arthur.

'Well, I suggest you speak to your grandfather right now to let him know you are all right, and that you are here!' Willbury insisted. All the eyes in the room fixed on Arthur and the doll. 'And when you have spoken to your grandfather, I should like to talk to him, if I may?' asked Willbury.

Arthur nodded. He wound the tiny handle on the box on the front of the doll. There was a gentle crackling noise, and then Grandfather's voice broke through.

'Arthur, Arthur, are you out there?'

'Yes! Yes! It's me! Grandfather, it's me! Arthur!' Arthur yelped. It was such a relief to hear Grandfather's voice.

'Arthur! Where are you? I've been so worried. Are you all right?' Grandfather's voice sounded shaky.

'I followed the cheese hunt like you told me to. I did try to be careful, Grandfather, but the huntsmen tried to catch me . . . They took my wings! And sealed up the drain! But I've escaped and found a safe place . . . and someone who can help me!' Arthur reassured him. 'I'm in an old shop, with a man called Willbury. He wants to speak to you.'

'Certainly—please pass the doll to him,' Grandfather told Arthur. Arthur gave the doll to Willbury, who had been looking at it a little uneasily. Willbury cleared his throat.

'Good evening, sir'

'Good evening, sir. This is Willbury Nibble speaking. I have Arthur with me in my home. I haven't heard the full story, but it sounds as if he has had a terrible time. I would just like to say that you have my word as a gentleman, that while your grandson is in my charge I shall do all within my power to keep him safe. I shall also endeavour to help him return to you, as soon as maybe!'

'Thank you, Mr Nibble!' replied Grandfather. 'If you could help Arthur get back to me safely, I would be very grateful!'

Arthur moved closer to the doll. 'Grandfather, how am I going to get back now that the huntsmen have blocked up the drain?'

For a moment there was just a gentle hissing and crackling from the doll, then they heard Grandfather's voice again. 'I know there are other routes between the town and the Underworld. But I don't know where they are. They belong to other creatures.' His voice sounded sad.

'Sir,' replied Willbury, 'I have a number of boxtrolls and a cabbagehead living with me. They may know of a way!'

Willbury looked up and was met by nodding heads. Even Titus had come out of hiding and was nodding.

'Yes! It seems they do,' said Willbury. 'I will have them help us guide Arthur back to you!'

'Thank you!' came the voice from the doll.

Arthur looked at the creatures gratefully. Of course—it was such a simple answer. He needn't have been so worried. Then Willbury spoke again.

'I think it might be a bit risky with these blackguards who chased Arthur roaming about. I suggest we wait till early tomorrow morning, then Fish and the others can find Arthur a hole.'

'I agree, Mr Nibble. I think Arthur has had enough excitement for one evening.' Then the voice from the doll paused for a moment. 'Getting Arthur back is my first concern. But I am worried about his wings. Without them he won't be able to collect food for us safely . . . '

'I understand your concern, sir. I am not sure where they are or how we might get them back, but I will think on it. It's getting late now, so I suggest that we all get some sleep. Do you have enough food for the moment?' asked Willbury.

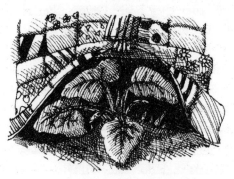

'I have several large clumps of rhubarb'

'Yes, I have several large clumps of rhubarb, growing under the bed,' said Grandfather.

'Good. We'll give Arthur a good supper, and there is plenty of space for him to sleep here.'

'Thank you so much, Mr Nibble. And Arthur, look after yourself . . . I need you back!' said Grandfather.

'I will, Grandfather. Goodnight,' replied Arthur.

'Goodnight, Arthur, and I shall see you in the morning.'

The doll fell silent, and Arthur took it back from Willbury. He kissed it and tucked it in his under-suit.

'Why don't we have a little something to eat, and Arthur can finish telling us his story,' Willbury suggested, looking at Arthur. Then, turning to Titus, he said, 'Titus. Get the big forks!'

A huge smile shot across Titus's face, and he disappeared back inside the barrel for a moment. He returned carrying massive three-foot forks and brought them over to Willbury. Willbury leant down and Titus whispered in his ear.

'Yes, Titus! Go and get the buns . . . and the cocoa bucket.' Willbury nodded.

Titus bounded out of the door at the back of the shop and returned carrying a huge plate of buns and a large zinc-plated bucket full of cocoa. He set them by the fire and the other creatures, Willbury, and Arthur gathered around him. Willbury hung the bucket on a hook over the fire and after a few minutes it was slowly bubbling. Everybody took a fork and started to toast the buns. When the buns were crisp, they dipped them in the cocoa before eating them.

Arthur finished his story as they ate. He told of how he would come up every night to gather food, but of how as it was a Sunday he had to go 'gardening'. Then rather shamefacedly he told of his raid on the greenhouse and how he had been struck by the woman, of his flight to the Cheese Hall, and how he had seen the hunt, and how he had tried to spy on them, then all that had followed—his wings breaking, the evil leader of the hunt, the hounds, and how he had escaped over the wall into the lane.

The boxtrolls listened in awe as they sucked on their buns, and Titus got so caught up in the story that he hid behind Willbury when Arthur mentioned the hounds. Arthur finished his tale and looked towards Willbury, who was staring into the fire.

'It has been quite an adventure, Arthur. I think we should get to bed,' said Willbury. 'Let's just finish off the cocoa.'

Willbury took the cocoa off the fire. When it had cooled a little they took it in turns to drink straight from the bucket. Arthur felt much better.

Drinking cocoa straight from the bucket

'Now, let's get our heads down. We need to be bright and fresh for the morning!' said Willbury.

The creatures found places for themselves around the room and nestled down. Willbury made up a bed for Arthur under the shop counter, out of old velvet curtains. Arthur

took off his hat and climbed in. Willbury tucked another
curtain around him.

'You sleep well, Arthur. I have an idea where we might
make enquiries about your wings.'

Willbury left Arthur to settle and the light in the shop
went out. Arthur pulled the soft velvet covers over his head.
The curtain felt heavy and gave off rather a comforting dusty
smell. Arthur lay quietly in the darkness and started
to think. It will be good to get back to Grandfather
tomorrow . . . But my wings . . . I can't lose those . . . I
wonder what Willbury meant when he said he had an idea?

His thoughts became slower as sleep overtook him. Soon
all that could be heard was gentle snoring.

Soon all that could be heard was gentle snoring

Snatcher

Snatcher raised the pole

Chapter 6

THE CEREMONY

Across the town from where Arthur slept, deep within the heart of the Cheese Hall, the huntsmen and their mounts were getting changed. All stripped down to their long johns, and hung their outer garments on pegs. From cases that were stored under the benches that bordered the room they took out outlandish furry capes, hats, and some battered musical instruments. They donned the clothes, picked up the instruments, and then made their way through a small wooden door into a large hexagonal chamber. This was some twenty feet across, about thirty feet high, with a vaulted ceiling. In the centre of the floor was a deep circular hole. If one had looked into the hole, one might have seen a bubbling mass of sticky yellow cheese far below. This was the Fondue Pit.

Watching from a balcony, about halfway up one wall, was Snatcher. He was dressed in the same furry robes and hat as the other huntsmen, but in his hand he held a wooden pole.

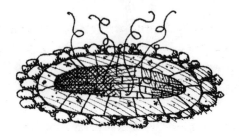

The Fondue Pit

At its tip was a gilded duck. A piece of string went from the
duck's head to Snatcher's hand. When the huntsmen had settled
down, Snatcher raised the pole and waved it slowly over his
head. The huntsmen started to play on their instruments.
Some had drums and others strange horns. The noise was
awful and grew louder and louder, till Snatcher pointed his
duck stick at the hole, and pulled the string. The huntsmen
immediately stopped playing. The duck's mouth opened and
emitted an eerie quack. The quack faded away, leaving only
the sound of bubbling molten cheese. Snatcher spoke.

'Members of the Guild, we are on our way to wreaking
revenge on this appalling town. Soon we will be unstoppable!'

The men assembled in the chamber cheered. Snatcher
raised his duck stick and the crowd grew silent.

'It is time to feed the Great One! . . . Gristle, lower the
cage,' Snatcher's voice boomed.

The duck stick

From somewhere above there was a clanking of chains, and the bleating of a cheese. Slowly a cage came into view. In it was one of the cheeses gathered from the hunt. The crowd watched in silence as the cage went lower and lower until it disappeared into the pit. After a few more seconds the bleating became more frenzied. Then suddenly it stopped, and the chain went slack.

There was another clank from high above, the chain tightened, and slowly an empty cage emerged from the pit. A few strands of cheese stretched, then broke from the bottom of the cage.

Snatcher raised the duck stick. Again it opened its mouth and quacked.

'More cheese, Mr Gristle!' Snatcher intoned.

Slowly a cage came into view

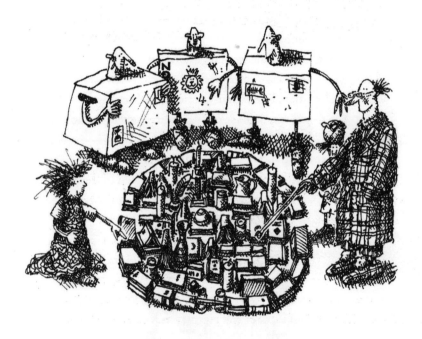

A model of Ratbridge

He sat up and banged his head

Chapter 7

WHICH HOLE?

Arthur woke up with a start. He sat up and banged his head on the wooden shelf above him. Then he remembered where he was. Pale daylight filled the space between the counter and the wall behind it. A face popped into view, and smiled at him.

'Good morning, Fish!' Arthur said, rubbing his head.

Fish gurgled in a friendly way and disappeared. He returned a moment later carrying the cocoa bucket. Arthur swung himself from under the counter and took the bucket.

He returned a moment later carrying the cocoa bucket

It had only a couple of inches of the rich dark liquid in the bottom. Obviously, he realized, he must be the last one up. He lifted the bucket and drank the lot. Fish giggled, then took the bucket back. Arthur wiped his mouth on the hem of his string vest and burped.

'Thank you. I needed that.'

Willbury appeared behind the counter wearing a worn dressing gown of green silk.

'Good morning, Arthur. I think we had better get ready. It's still early, but it's market day, so the streets will get busy quite soon, and I know the underlings prefer it when there are not many people about.'

'We have made a model of the town'

Arthur stood up, followed Willbury and Fish out from behind the counter, and almost walked into a pile of books. Arthur looked down to see a complex pattern of books covering most of the floor. The other creatures stood around its edges.

'What's this?' asked Arthur.

'It's Ratbridge,' replied Willbury. 'My friends here don't really understand maps, so we have made a model of the town with all its buildings and streets. This way we can plan our expedition.'

Arthur looked again at the books on the floor. There before him lay every street and building, defined by books and other objects from the shop. It was astonishing! He looked about and got his bearings. Then he pointed to a small dictionary. 'That's where we are!'

'Yes!' laughed Willbury. 'It works quite well, doesn't it?'

'Well, where have we got to go?'

The underlings started chattering, and each of them pointed at a different part of the 'town'. There seemed to be some difference of opinion.

'The underlings all have favourite holes,' said Willbury. 'I think that we will have to work this out.' He then addressed the underlings. 'I will give each of you a six groat coin, and I want you to place it where your hole is.'

Willbury took a small leather bag from out of his pocket and handed each of the underlings a shiny silver coin. The creatures then carefully leaned over the model of Ratbridge and placed their coins. Willbury surveyed the positions of the holes.

Willbury handed each of the underlings a shiny silver coin

'I rather like the idea of Titus's hole. It's nice and close,' he finally declared. The boxtrolls all laughed. Willbury looked at them, puzzled.

'What is it? What's wrong with Titus's hole?' he asked.

The boxtrolls squeaked and made signs at Arthur and Titus.

'Oh, of course,' said Willbury. 'Titus's hole would be too small for Arthur.' He turned to Titus. Titus reluctantly nodded.

Willbury turned to the boxtrolls. 'Well then, what do you suggest?' Fish seemed the most insistent. He kept pointing at his coin, which was placed amongst books that made the shape of houses and gardens near the edge of town.

Willbury's eyes traced a route from the shop to Fish's coin. 'It seems to me that Fish may have a point. Arthur should have no trouble getting down a boxtroll hole . . . And we could get there very quietly down these back streets.' Willbury indicated the route with a walking stick. 'If we find there are too many people about we can always divert and make our way to one of the other holes. We'll set off right after breakfast.' He turned to Arthur. 'I am sure your grandfather is anxious to see you again.'

Arthur paused. 'But what about my wings?'

'Yes . . . well . . . ' replied Willbury. 'I told you I had an idea. Based on what you said about the man who took them, it occurred to me that he must be someone who knows about mechanical things and the like. I know a person who knows most people in that line. Finding her may take some time as I have not seen her about recently, so I think it better that we get you back to your grandfather first.'

The creatures placed their coins

Arthur's heart sank. 'I am not sure how I am going to be able to collect food for Grandfather if I haven't got wings.'

'Well, you don't need to worry about that. I'll go to the market this morning and get you some food. I have to go anyway as we are out of buns!' Willbury looked around indulgently at the creatures. He turned back to Arthur. 'Come back tonight and I will have plenty for you to take back to the Underworld.'

Then Willbury gave Arthur a rather disapproving look. 'Mind you, I don't hold with taking other people's things. None of this would have happened if you hadn't helped yourself to that lady's bananas. Now, everybody collect up these books and put everything away, and I'll make breakfast.'

'I don't hold with taking other people's things'

Arthur, the boxtrolls, and Titus set about tidying the floor. When they had finished they hovered round the fireplace where Willbury was using the cocoa bucket to make porridge.

'I am afraid it may taste a little chocolatey,' apologized Willbury.

'I think I should rather like that,' replied Arthur, and the other creatures nodded in agreement.

Willbury grinned. 'Well, then I shall add more cocoa and sugar. It will cut out the need to make cocoa afterwards. Titus, would you be so good as to fetch the bowls and spoons?'

After finishing the cocoa porridge, which everyone declared a success, Willbury disappeared into the back room for a few moments, and reappeared dressed. Then he unbolted the front door, and the little band set off through the deserted streets.

Willbury was using the cocoa bucket to make porridge

The group made its way through the back streets of Ratbridge

At each corner the boxtrolls checked for humans

Chapter 8

SEARCH FOR A HOLE

The boxtrolls trotted ahead as the group made its way through the back streets of Ratbridge. At each corner the boxtrolls checked for humans, then waved the group on. As yet they had the town to themselves. When they passed a carpentry workshop, Willbury pointed to some blue chalk marks on the cobbles.

The boxtrolls trotted ahead

'I think Fish has been here recently,' he said to Arthur. Arthur's eyes followed the direction of the arrow drawn on the floor. It pointed to a pale strip of brickwork where a drainpipe had once been fixed. 'Yes, I really must have words with them,' Willbury added.

The group moved on. Within ten minutes they were approaching the site of Fish's hole.

Fish, taking the lead, stopped by a door in a garden wall.

He signed to the others to keep quiet and follow him. He pushed at the door and they all made their way into an overgrown garden. It was clear that the house that it belonged to was deserted. Everyone followed Fish up the garden path, carefully avoiding brambles. He led the way to a brick outhouse, and opened its door. Then he let out an anguished squeak.

Fish stopped by a door in a garden wall

The others crowded round to see what had upset him. A large rusty iron plate covered the floor inside. Some kind of dried black glue bulged from around its edges.

Fish turned to them and started to make gobbling noises.

'Confound it!' said Willbury. Then he looked at the boxtrolls. Shoe and Egg were comforting Fish.

Some kind of dried black glue bulged from around its edges

'Let's see if we can lift it,' said Willbury. 'If we get a large stick we could try to force it under the edge.'

Arthur spotted an old spade in the brambles, and hurried to fetch it. Willbury smiled.

An old spade

'Good thinking, Arthur. I think Fish is the strongest one here. Give him the spade, and let him try.'

Arthur handed the spade to Fish, who tried to push it

He made no impression

under the edge of the iron plate. But the glue was so hard that even after a great deal of effort he made no impression.

'I don't think we should worry too much, Fish. The hole must have been found when someone was doing repairs on the house, and they just covered it up,' said Willbury consolingly. 'Let's try another hole.'

Fish frowned. He threw the spade down in a rather bad-tempered way.

'Fish! That is not the sort of behaviour I expect from a boxtroll. Pick that up and leave it neatly against the wall, please,' Willbury said sternly.

Fish looked huffy, but did what he was told.

'Shoe, I think your hole is the closest one to here. Let's go there,' Willbury continued. Then he put his hand on Arthur's shoulder. 'Don't worry. We'll have you back home before you can say Jack Robinson.'

The group set off again, this time following Shoe. Fish trailed behind, muttering to himself and kicking every pebble he found in his path.

The butcher's shop

They passed through a few more streets, then arrived outside a butcher's shop. Shoe led them up the side alley next to the shop, and into a walled yard. On one side was a derelict pigsty. Shoe looked about to check that nobody was watching them, then opened the pigsty's gate and went inside. He came back out looking worried. He took Willbury's hand, and led him into the sty. Arthur and the others followed. Old straw had been pushed up around the edges of the sty revealing another large iron plate.

'Oh dear!' muttered Willbury. 'This looks bad. Two holes both sealed up!'

'Three if you count mine,' said Arthur.

'You're right, Arthur. This seems more than a coincidence,' said Willbury, sounding worried.

Arthur was also starting to feel worried. He moved forward and took a long look at the iron plate. 'This is how the huntsmen sealed up my hole last night.' Suddenly getting home did not seem so straightforward after all.

On one side was a derelict pigsty

'I'm beginning to suspect these things could be connected. We had better go and check the other holes forthwith,' said a perturbed Willbury.

Egg now came forward and gurgled to Willbury.

'Yes, Egg! Let's check your hole. Hopefully we'll have more luck there.'

They left the pigsty and emerged up the alley onto the street. A few people were now out and about, pushing handcarts towards the market. They didn't seem to pay any attention to Arthur, Willbury, and the creatures, but the

boxtrolls looked uneasy. And Titus nervously tried to keep Arthur between himself and the humans.

Egg led them to a rubbish heap behind the Glue Works, where he immediately started pulling pieces of junk away from one end of the heap. After a few moments he stopped. Sunlight glinted off an iron plate . . .

In silence Egg turned and looked back at them. The boxtrolls started to make an agitated mewing sound. Willbury walked over to the iron plate and stared. Arthur joined him, feeling increasingly alarmed.

'Why would anyone do this?' he asked.

'I am not sure . . . but I have got a very bad feeling about it. We should check Titus's hole to see if the same thing has happened there.' Willbury turned and spoke to Titus, who was trembling all over. 'Can you show us your hole, please?'

Titus nodded his head and the group set off again, this time at a real pace. The streets were now filling but although the boxtrolls still seemed very nervous of the passers-by, and tried to keep to the shadows, Arthur noticed that in fact nobody seemed to take much notice of them at all. Titus was so concerned about getting to his hole that he hardly noticed the onlookers, and even dared to lead them.

They went up and down so many streets that Arthur wasn't sure where they were any more. Titus moved more and more quickly. Then he disappeared around a corner into an alley. The others turned the corner to see Titus in the distance, running towards a drain. Before he reached it, he stopped.

The sun was glinting off a large iron sheet covering the drain. The others caught up, to find Titus whimpering to himself. This time, for several seconds no one said a word.

Titus hardly noticed the onlookers

Finally, Willbury spoke. 'I'm so sorry, Arthur, but I am not sure what I can do. This is terrible . . . and I don't think we know of any more holes.'

Arthur did not know what to say. The thought of never going home again was too much to bear.

Willbury took Arthur's hand and gave it a squeeze. The underlings stood in silence and stared at the iron plate. Then Fish made a noise.

'GeeeGoooW!'

The other boxtrolls turned to look at him and repeated the noise. 'GeeeGoooW! GeeeGoooW! GeeeGoooW!'

Fish turned to Willbury and started to jump up and

down, suddenly filled with energy again. The other boxtrolls joined in. Even Titus was nodding eagerly.

'GeeeeGooow!'

'What is it?' asked Willbury.

The underlings all pointed down the street.

Willbury perked up. 'I think they know of another hole, Arthur.'

The underlings nodded.

'Well, let's go!' said Willbury. And they set off at a trot.

The wet dry dock

A fresh-water sea-cow

Chapter 9

THE WET DRY DOCK

Not far from the back of the Cheese Hall was a disused dry dock. This was connected to the canal by a short channel. It was no longer dry as its huge wooden gates were open and hanging from their hinges. The hulks of several narrow boats were partially submerged in the murky water that filled it, and the occasional bubble rose up and broke the weedy surface. If you listened very carefully you might have heard a low rumbling mooing sound coming from its depths.

Willbury and Arthur looked expectantly at the boxtrolls. The boxtrolls stared into the water. Then more bubbles broke the surface. The boxtrolls grinned and started to clap their hands excitedly. Fish looked up and down the footpath and spotted a clump of grass. He ran to it, pulled it up, and tossed it into the water, near where the bubbles had emerged. It sank slowly. And just as slowly, something large moved under the water.

Fish spotted a clump of grass

Arthur was startled. 'Quick, Willbury! Did you see that?'

'Yes I did . . . I'm not sure what it is.'

Fish, Shoe, and Egg were now running up and down the bank, gathering vegetation. When they had built a small heap they nodded to each other, gathered it up, and threw it in the water. Some of it sank, but most of it floated. They all waited.

A large hairy pink muzzle broke the surface of the water, right in the middle of the floating vegetation.

'Oh my word!' said Willbury. 'I have never seen one of those before.'

Something large moved under the water

A large hairy pink muzzle broke the surface of the water

'What is it? What is it?' Arthur asked impatiently.

'I believe it is a fresh-water sea-cow!'

The boxtrolls nodded. The fresh-water sea-cow lifted its head above the water, revealing two large gentle eyes and a pair of short horns. The creature was huge. Arthur stared in awe at its large black and white body floating beneath the water. It started to vacuum up the greenery with its huge floppy nose. With a couple of breathy sucks the food was gone. The sea-cow sank back down till only its eyes and horns were visible above the water. It looked very sad.

Fish held out some dandelion leaves

Fish crept closer to the water's edge, crouched down and held out some dandelion leaves. Slowly the sea-cow moved towards him, raised its head, and sucked in the leaves. Fish's hand got covered in slobber, but he kept very still. Then very carefully he reached out with his other hand and patted the sea-cow's nose. The group watched in silence.

Fish now made gentle gurgling noises as he patted the pink muzzle, and the sea-cow held still. Then it let out a deep sigh. Fish made a mewing sound and the sea-cow replied with another sigh.

Fish's hand got covered in slobber

Arthur tugged on Willbury's arm. 'I think he's talking to it!'

They watched for a few minutes as the boxtroll and the sea-cow made conversation. Then the sea-cow sank back into the water and disappeared. Bubbles rose from the pool and then all was still.

Fish stood back up. He looked very upset.

'What is it, Fish?' asked Willbury.

Fish started to jabber. As he did so, Willbury leaned

down, and Titus began whispering in his ear. Arthur realized that Titus was translating what Fish was saying to Willbury.

Willbury looked more and more uneasy. When Fish had finished Willbury turned to Arthur.

'Something tragic has happened. That poor sea-cow!' Willbury's voice trailed off.

'What is it?' asked Arthur quietly.

'Well, the fresh-water sea-cows live in waterways under the town. They use a tunnel that extends from the dry dock to come out into the canal to feed. That sea-cow has three calves. A few days ago she left them here to play while she went off to forage in the canal. When she returned the calves were gone . . . and the tunnel blocked . . . '

Fish slowly nodded his head. The group stood very still.

'What can we do?' asked Arthur.

'I'm not sure, Arthur. I'm not sure,' said Willbury very quietly. Then he turned to the underlings. 'Do you know of any more holes?'

The underlings slowly shook their heads.

Willbury gazed into the water of the dock for a while then spoke. 'I really have no idea what is going on. I think it best if we all go back to the shop.'

He started to walk back up the path. The others followed in silence. As they trailed through the now crowded streets, Titus gripped Arthur's hand. Things did not look good.

Willbury

'Grandfather! Are you there?'

Chapter 10

THE RETURN

As soon as they were inside the shop Willbury turned to Arthur. 'I think we had better call your grandfather. He needs to know what's going on.' Arthur nodded in agreement.

He reached under his shirt and took out the doll, wound the handle, and soon the familiar crackling could be heard.

'Grandfather! Are you there?'

Grandfather's voice came back straight away.

'Arthur, where are you? Are you underground yet?'

'No . . . I am not,' Arthur replied. 'We have tried, but all the underlings' holes have been blocked up.'

There was a pause. Then they heard Grandfather again.

'Where are you now?'

'I am back at the shop with Mr Nibble.'

'Can you let me speak to him, please?'

Arthur passed the doll to Willbury.

'Every entrance has been sealed up'

'Hello, sir,' said Willbury.

'Hello, Mr Nibble . . . this doesn't sound good at all. Have you any idea what is going on?'

'Frankly . . . no. We have tried five entrances to the Underworld, and every one has been sealed up. With Arthur's that makes six.'

'Do you think that lot who chased Arthur last night are sealing the holes to stop Arthur getting back underground?'

'I don't think so. Some of the holes have been sealed up for some time. It's not just about Arthur and his wings.'

There was another pause.

'Do you have any clue who this bunch of ruffians who chased Arthur were?' asked Grandfather.

Willbury thought for a moment. 'I don't, but there is someone I know who is well up in the world of inventions. She knows everyone with an interest in mechanics in Ratbridge. She might know the man who took Arthur's wings.'

'If you could follow that lead up I would be very grateful.'

'I have to go to the market for food, and will go to find my friend after that,' replied Willbury.

There was another silence. Then Grandfather spoke again.

'This business with the cheese hunting? It's been illegal for years now. In the old days it was the Cheese Guild that did the hunting, but the Guild was said to have died out when the trade was banned.'

'Do you think it might be something to do with that?' asked Willbury.

'Years ago, when I lived above ground, there were rumours about the Cheese Guild. Nothing specific . . . just the odd story of "Goings On" . . . secret meetings and the like.'

There was a long pause

Willbury looked quizzical. 'If you don't mind me asking—why do you live underground?'

There was a long pause. When Grandfather finally replied, there was a steely tone to his voice that Arthur had never heard before. 'I was accused of a crime that I did not commit. I have had to take refuge here ever since.'

Arthur felt his skin prickle as he stared at the doll. This was the closest he had ever come to finding out the reason for their life underground. Would Grandfather say more? What sort of crime could have driven him underground for so long? He looked up and found Willbury's gaze upon him. Then Grandfather continued.

'I have kept it from Arthur as I felt he was too young to understand. But please believe me when I say you have my word as a gentleman that I am an innocent man.'

'I believe you, sir,' said Willbury. Then looking at Arthur he spoke again. 'We shall leave it at that. I think Arthur may be old enough to understand. But I also think it better he hears this sort of thing from you face to face.'

'Thank you,' came the voice from the doll.

Willbury looked at Arthur one more time, then asked another question. 'On a more immediate matter. Do you have enough food, Grandfather?'

'Yes. The rhubarb seems to be thriving. I think I have a few days' supply.'

'Well, hopefully we can get this matter sorted out very quickly. I am sure Arthur will be back with you soon.'

'I do hope so,' said Arthur quietly.

'Yes . . . We will go and see my friend this morning. I am sure she will be able to help,' said Willbury.

'Can you call me as soon as you know anything?'

'I will make sure that Arthur calls you as soon as we have any information.'

'Thank you . . . And, Arthur, YOU TAKE CARE . . . I need you back.'

'All right, Grandfather!' said Arthur. He took the doll from Willbury. 'I will be very careful . . . and I will be back . . . Soon!'

Arthur was trying to sound positive, but actually he felt very unsure now of when he was going to get home—if ever.

'Speak to you later then,' said Grandfather.

'Goodbye . . . till later!' Arthur put the doll away.

'Right!' said Willbury firmly. 'I think we need a good feed. I can always think better on a full stomach. Let's draw up a shopping list.'

Arthur could tell that Willbury was as worried as he was, but that he was trying to keep everyone's spirits up. If he could put a brave face on the situation, then Arthur would too. The boxtrolls and Titus needed him to be strong, so he tried to raise a smile as they all sat down around the shop. Willbury took out a quill and a scrap of paper from under his chair.

Then there was a knock.

Willbury took out a quill and a scrap of paper

A rather grubby man

Everyone turned to the door

Chapter 11

A VISIT

Everyone turned to the door. Through the window they could see the tall shadow of a figure standing outside.

Willbury put his finger to his mouth. 'Quiet!' he whispered. 'It may be the hunters looking for Arthur. Arthur, quick, hide behind the counter.'

Arthur obeyed without hesitation. He never wanted to see the huntsmen again if he could help it. The memory of their leader's sneering face still made him shudder. He got back down into the space where he had slept the night before. There was a crack in the woodwork, and by placing his eye close to it he could still see the shop door. He watched as Willbury unlocked the door and stepped back.

A rather grubby man wearing a frock coat and a top hat stood on the doorstep. He was holding a large box in his arms, and on the ground by his side was a bucket.

A bucket

'Excuse me, sir,' he said in an oily voice. 'My name is Gristle, and I represent the Northgate Miniature Livestock Company. I was wondering if you might be interested in buying some rather small creatures?'

Willbury looked quizzically at the box, and then stared at the bucket. 'Er. Umm. You know this is not a pet shop any more?' he said slowly. 'What are they?'

'They are the very latest thing! Miniatures! Little versions of some of the pet industry's best sellers.'

Mr Gristle put down the box and, with a flourish, took off the lid. Willbury took a look at the contents of the box, and couldn't help smiling.

'They're beautiful!' he said, squatting down. Then he frowned. 'But they don't seem very happy.'

'No,' replied Gristle. 'I think it's a by-product of the breeding.'

The underlings had become curious. They moved shyly closer to have a look.

'You wouldn't like to do a swap, would you?'

'You wouldn't like to do a swap, would you? I'm looking for BIG creatures,' Gristle said, eyeing up Willbury's companions. All the big creatures pulled away again, and hid behind Willbury.

All the big creatures hid behind Willbury

'Certainly not!' Willbury blurted, outraged. Then his curiosity got the better of him. 'What's in the bucket?'

Arthur was also immensely curious, but couldn't see what was happening now as Willbury and the underlings were obscuring his view. He would have to wait, he told himself.

Willbury took out his leather coin bag

'A little spotty swimming thing. I believe it's from Peru,' said Gristle.

'How much do you want for them?' asked Willbury.

'How would five groats sound?' said Gristle, rather hopefully.

'It would sound very expensive!' replied Willbury.

'Well, three groats, five farthings. It's my last offer. I can always take them to the pie shop,' Gristle smirked.

Willbury looked shocked. The underlings gasped collectively. Willbury took out his leather coin bag and gave Gristle the money.

'Thank you, squire! Are you sure you don't want to part with any of your BIG friends?' Gristle asked again.

'Absolutely not! Now, be off with you!' Willbury had taken a distinct dislike to Mr Gristle. He lifted the box and the bucket into the shop, and closed the door on the salesman.

The letterbox flipped open.

'I really am very interested in your BIG friends, sir. I'm sure we could come to some arrangement?' said the disembodied voice of Mr Gristle.

'Go AWAY!' said Willbury, starting to get angry.

The letterbox closed for a moment, and then a ten groat banknote appeared, held by two long thin grubby fingers.

'Pretty please,' whispered Gristle.

The fingers started to wave the note. Willbury took a lone cucumber from the vegetable box that was kept on the floor.

'I'm warning you. GO AWAY! I do not sell friends!' Willbury was turning red.

Another banknote held by another pair of fingers slipped through the letterbox, and started waving.

'Oh, go on!'

'Oh, go on! Twenty groats. They are only dumb old underlings,' the voice said.

This was too much for Willbury. He raised the cucumber and brought it down on the letterbox flap. There was a 'Splut!' as the cucumber hit the flap, a 'Snap!' as the flap closed on the fingers, and a scream from outside. The fingers and the banknotes disappeared.

'You'll be sorry for this!' came a muffled shout from outside. Then they heard the sound of footsteps hurrying away.

A silence fell over the shop. Willbury turned and spoke. 'You can come out now, Arthur.'

Arthur joined the group huddled around the box and bucket

Arthur joined the group huddled around the box and bucket. He peered into the box. The bottom was covered with straw, with half a turnip, covered in tiny bite marks, lying in one corner. Standing amongst the straw were a number of tiny creatures. There was a cabbagehead and a boxtroll, both about five inches high, and three trotting badgers. Most trotting badgers were the size of large dogs, but these were the size of mice. All the creatures in the box were shaking with fear.

Three trotting badgers

Fish leaned over the box, and made a low, cooing noise. The tiny boxtroll looked up and started squeaking. Fish looked puzzled. He looked up at Shoe and Egg, who also seemed puzzled. It was obviously a boxtroll, but they couldn't understand what it was saying. Shoe grunted softly. Fish nodded, raced out of the room, then raced back in again. In his hand was a brass nut and bolt. He laid them in the straw next to the tiny boxtroll. The tiny boxtroll made some more squeaking sounds, then picked up the nut and bolt, kissed them and gave them a hug. The big boxtrolls smiled.

The tiny boxtroll

A small splash came from the bucket. Everyone turned to see ripples spreading over the surface of the murky green water.

'I wonder?' Willbury muttered to himself.

He reached for a small piece of the shattered cucumber, and dropped it into the bucket. For a moment it hung just below the surface. Then a tiny head emerged from the murk and started to nibble the cucumber. As the creature fed, more of it came into view. Its body was short and stout, a bit like a very small seal. It had horns and a large floppy nose, and its skin was white with black patches.

'Oh my!' said Willbury. 'It's a tiny fresh-water sea-cow.'

'It's so small!' said Arthur. 'You don't think it's one of the calves the mother lost?'

'No, no. They would be much bigger than this,' Willbury said. Then he muttered to himself. 'Peru, did he say? I didn't think that they had them in South America.'

He looked up at Fish. 'Will you and Titus go and get the old fish tank, from the back of the shop? Fill it with fresh water. We need to get this little one out of the dirty bucket.'

The sea-cow started to explore its new home

Fish and Titus fetched the tank and placed it on the counter, then started to fill it with jugs of water. Willbury laid an old stoneware jar on its side in the tank. There was some pondweed in the bucket, so he took that out and placed it in the tank too. When the tank was three quarters full, Willbury told Fish and Titus to stop. Then he lifted the bucket onto the counter, rolled up his sleeves, and gently lifted the sea-cow out into the tank. With a plop the little creature entered the water. It swam straight to the bottom of the tank and disappeared into the jar. They all stood around the tank and watched. After a minute or so, a nose emerged.

'Keep very still,' said Arthur quietly. He was practically holding his breath, not wanting to disturb the tiny creature.

Slowly the sea-cow swam out and started to explore its new home.

'Now we must find homes for our other friends,' Willbury said. 'I want Fish, Shoe, and Egg to look after the little boxtroll, and Titus, you can look after the tiny cabbagehead.'

The big boxtrolls looked very happy. Willbury picked up the little boxtroll (who was still hugging the nut and bolt) and passed him to Fish. The other boxtrolls crowded around. After a great deal of billing and cooing they set off around the shop to give their new friend a tour.

Titus looked nervous. Willbury lifted the tiny cabbagehead up to his nose. He took a sniff and smiled, then offered it to Titus to smell. Titus leant forward and took a tiny sniff.

Willbury picked up the little boxtroll

After a moment a smile spread over his face too. He then lowered his face to the tiny cabbagehead and allowed it to smell him. The tiny cabbagehead gave a little squeak, and jumped onto Titus's shoulder.

'Why don't you show him where you live?' suggested Willbury.

Titus's eyes grew bright. He clutched the tiny cabbagehead to his chest, shot across the room, and disappeared through the hole in his barrel.

Willbury smiled. 'Titus really needed a companion!'

Suddenly there was a scuffling from the box and the trotting badgers scurried across the floor and disappeared into a mouse hole in the skirting board.

'Oh dear!' said Willbury.

Arthur picked up the box and turned it over. One corner had been chewed away, leaving a small hole.

'That's the problem with trotting badgers! They are really wild . . . and have REALLY sharp teeth,' said Arthur. 'Grandfather always warned me to stay away from the outer caves and tunnels where they live. He says "You can get in real trouble with a trotting badger!"'

'Oh! Well, do you think these little ones will be all right?' asked Willbury.

Titus with the tiny cabbagehead

'If they are anything like the big ones they should have no problems. It's the mice in that hole that I feel sorry for . . . trotting badgers will eat anything.'

'Well, we'll leave out some milk and biscuits for them later. Maybe if we keep them fed they'll leave the mice alone. I don't think there is anything else we can do,' said Willbury looking at the hole in the skirting board.

He turned and picked up the quill and paper from his chair. 'Now I think we should finish this shopping list, get to the market, and then find my friend.'

Arthur and Willbury sat down again. As soon as the boxtrolls realized what was going on they joined them.

'How are you getting on with your new friend?' he asked them.

Fish gurgled and pointed at a matchbox on the mantelpiece, then at the little boxtroll who Shoe was now holding.

'Oh! You have called him "Match". How very appropriate,' said Willbury.

The boxtrolls and Arthur giggled.

'Now what would everybody like to eat?' asked Willbury.

Shoe nudged Egg, who then reached inside his box somewhere and produced a folded piece of paper. He handed it to Willbury. Arthur watched as Willbury unfolded it. Drawn very neatly on the paper were pictures of all the foods that the boxtrolls wanted, grouped together by type.

'Thank you, Egg!' said Willbury, studying the pictures. 'I notice that you are rather light on vegetables. You know they are good for you.'

The boxtrolls moaned. Willbury turned towards the barrel in the corner. 'Titus! Could you come out? I think we need some help with the shopping list.'

Titus appeared, carrying the little cabbagehead, and took up position standing next to Willbury.

'So, Titus, do you have any suggestions for vegetables?'

The boxtrolls looked glum while Titus's eyes lit up. He leaned over and started to whisper in Willbury's ear.

Willbury was soon struggling to keep up. The list grew very long. The boxtrolls looked increasingly unhappy. Then Willbury raised a hand and Titus stopped.

'I think that is enough vegetables. Thank you, Titus.'

Titus looked at the little cabbagehead and whispered again to Willbury.

'Yes. I am sure I can get your friend a Brussels sprout.' Willbury caught the boxtrolls making faces at each other. 'You could take a few tips from cabbageheads on diet.' Willbury looked back down at the paper they had given him. 'Boxtrolls cannot live by . . . cake, biscuits, treacle, boiled sweets, toffee, shortbread, pasties, anchovies, pickled onions, raspberry jam, and lemonade . . . alone!'

The boxtrolls looked rather guilty. Willbury turned to Arthur. 'What would you like to eat?'

'We had better get off'

'Do you think we could have some more cocoa and buns?' he asked rather sheepishly.

Willbury raised one eyebrow. 'Well, only as part of a properly balanced diet . . . ' he began. Then he giggled. 'I was going to get them anyway.'

Arthur smiled.

'And I think I shall get myself a few pies . . . ' said Willbury, finishing the list and putting down his quill.

'Right, we had better get off. I think it best if we leave the underlings and their new friends here.'

Three men in top hats and mufflers, sitting on a large cart

Willbury put on his coat while Arthur stood waiting by the shop door. Arthur had never been to market, and he was rather excited by the idea. But when Willbury opened the door, there was an immediate shock. The street was thronging with people. Arthur was astonished. He had never been above ground in the middle of the day before. He never dreamed that there could be so many people in the world. Suddenly he felt rather frightened.

'Keep close, I don't want to lose you,' said Willbury.

And off they set.

What they failed to notice was that across the street were three men in top hats and mufflers, sitting on a large cart. As Willbury and Arthur headed towards the market, the men climbed down. One lifted a large metal bar from the back of the cart. The other two took out some old sacks. The men then walked shiftily towards the shop, all the time checking to see that nobody was watching them.

The men walked shiftily towards the shop

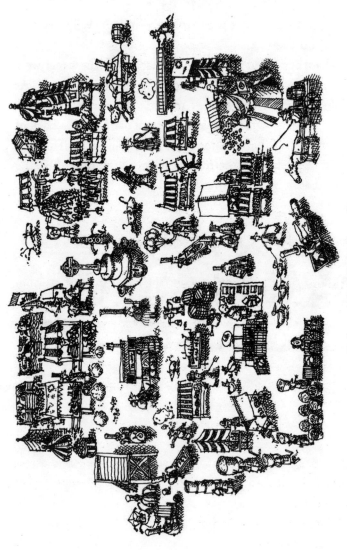

Early morning in Ratbridge market

Willbury led Arthur through the streets of Ratbridge

Chapter 12

THE MARKET

Willbury led Arthur through the streets of Ratbridge towards the market. Arthur had never been anywhere so crowded. There were tradesmen and women, farmers, shopkeepers, dogs, chickens, pigs, street sellers, buskers, and more children than he had ever seen in his life. On his night-time expeditions he had rarely seen children and when he had, he'd had to hide. But now they took no notice of him as they played. Some of them were kicking a leather ball the size of a cabbage about, while others were chasing each other, or fiddling with sticks in puddles. Arthur felt a little jealous at the easy way they laughed and spoke with each other.

'Willbury?' asked Arthur.

'Yes, Arthur?'

'What do children do?'

'You know. Play with friends, and go to school, and the like . . . '

Arthur was not sure he did know. He looked at the children. 'I don't think I have any friends.'

Willbury stopped and turned to him. 'I think you do! What about Fish . . . and Egg and Shoe . . . and Titus . . . and me?'

Arthur smiled, and they walked on. It was so noisy! There was shouting, barking, horses' hooves on cobblestones, the rumble of cartwheels, and over everything was the cackling of the ladies . . .

There were an awful lot of ladies doing an awful lot of cackling. And as they cackled, they tottered slowly down the streets, their bottoms wobbling behind them. Arthur had not seen bottoms like these before. From the way the ladies paraded their 'derrières' it seemed that to have an interesting behind was very much the thing! Round ones, cone-shaped ones, pyramidal ones, cuboid ones, and some that defied description. All large, and wobbling like jellies.

The ladies seemed perturbed by the bottoms of their rivals and kept taking furtive looks at the competing behinds. And they had plenty of time for these observations as they moved so slowly. This was because they wore ridiculously high shoes, which seemed to have been specially designed to make walking close to impossible.

Arthur could not help overhearing the conversation of two of the ladies.

There were an awful lot of ladies doing an awful lot of cackling

'Hark at her,' said one to another.

'Which one do you mean? That Ms Fox?' replied the other.

'Yes! Coming on hoity-toity with her new hexagonal buttocks,' said the first, with more than a hint of jealousy.

'No? And on shoes like that! She thinks she's the bee's knees, and she doesn't even realize that hessian went out weeks ago!'

Arthur had no idea what they were talking about. He looked up at Willbury, slightly bewildered. Willbury smiled, leaned towards him, and whispered, 'Fashion victims!'

Approaching the market the streets became more and more crowded. Arthur found it very exciting. As they entered the market square they were met by a wall of rather shabby people.

*As they entered the market square they were met by
a wall of rather shabby people*

'Hang on very tightly to my hand, Arthur!' said Willbury as he pushed into the throng.

Arthur grabbed Willbury's hand and hung on. Slowly they squeezed their way through the jostling mass of bodies. Arthur could see very little except when there was a break in the crowd and for a moment he would catch sight of the stalls . . . He was amazed! He had never seen such a profusion of things. Stacks of sausages, bundles of new and second-hand clothes, strange tools and gadgets, bottles of grim looking medicines, stacks of broken furniture, toys, clocks, pots and pans . . . The list went on and on. Even when he couldn't see much about him the smells kept flooding into his nostrils. Some were familiar, some new, some sweet and

some very, very unpleasant. Arthur felt boggled by it all. How strange the town seemed by day. Occasionally Willbury would guide them towards a stall where he would buy food, and then off they would set again on their journey. As the shopping amassed Arthur helped Willbury with the bags, which were making it increasingly harder to move through the market.

Finally they broke free of the crowds and Arthur found himself standing by the cross in the very centre of the market.

Willbury led him towards a pie stall which stood against the market cross. Around it was a group of people wearing oily overalls, chewing on pies, chatting, and drawing on blackboards attached to the stall. Built into one side of the stall was a strange copper drum with a chimney. A man behind the stall was shovelling coal into the drum through a door in its base.

Around it was a group of people wearing oily overalls, chewing on pies

'Are you hungry?' Willbury asked Arthur. 'The pies here are simply the best in Ratbridge. Would you like to try one?'

Arthur looked at the group around the stall tucking into their pies and decided that he was very hungry indeed.

'Yes, please!' he answered.

The man behind the stall looked up and smiled at Willbury.

'Good day to you, Mr Nibble, sir. Is it the usual? A nice turkey and ham special for yourself?' the man asked Willbury. 'And what would the young man like?'

'Yes, a turkey and ham would be very nice, thank you, Mr Whitworth,' replied Willbury. 'I recommend that you try one as well, Arthur.'

'Yes, please!' said Arthur again.

Mr Whitworth opened a door in the top of the copper drum and scooped out two large steaming pies with his spade. He flipped them onto a stack of newspapers on the counter, put down the spade and then wrapped a few sheets of the newspaper around the pies.

'Will there be anything else, Mr Nibble?' asked Mr Whitworth.

'Just a bit of information. I am trying to get in touch with Marjorie. Do you happen to know where she is?' replied Mr Willbury.

'Haven't you heard? She's been camping down at the Patent Hall for weeks, ever since they lost her application,' answered Mr Whitworth.

Mr Whitworth opened a door in the top of the copper drum and scooped out two large steaming pies with his spade

'Lost her application?' Willbury sounded alarmed.

'Yes. Marjorie took her application and prototype for some new invention of hers for approval, but the man who was checking them disappeared for lunch with them. And never came back . . . Now Marjorie's stuck there—if she leaves the queue she could lose her invention for ever!'

'How awful! We must go and see her straight away.' Willbury hesitated for a moment. 'I'll take her six of your finest pork and sage, please! She'll need to keep her strength up. How much is that?' asked Willbury, offering a silver coin.

'They are two groats each, Mr Nibble. But I'll not be taking your money. We are all doing what we can to help poor

Marjorie. It may be a small thing but pies are vital to keeping one together. If you take them down to the Hall for her I'll not be charging you for the pies for you and the boy either.'

Mr Whitworth pulled six more pies and a small cake from the oven, wrapped them, and then placed them in a sack with the two turkey and ham pies.

'The cake is for you, young man.' Mr Whitworth smiled and winked at Arthur.

'Thank you!' said Arthur.

'Yes! It is very kind of you, Mr Whitworth. Thank you indeed!' said Willbury.

Mr Whitworth pulled six more pies and a small cake from the oven, wrapped them, and then placed them in a sack with the two turkey and ham pies

Mr Whitworth passed the sack to Arthur. 'You look like a strong lad. If you run out of energy you can always eat one.'

Happily Arthur took the sack and swung it gently over his shoulder. Then with a parting wave to Mr Whitworth they picked up the shopping bags and set off into the crowd again.

IS THAT THEOREM CAUSING CONFUSION?
IS THAT HYPOTHESIS BEFUDDLING YOUR BRAIN?

You need brain food! Try a pie!!! From

WHITWORTH'S SCIENTIFIC PIES

Choose from today's finely-balanced range:

Turkey and ham

Turkey and ham in precisely equal quantities, with a catalyst
of four-sevenths of a teaspoon of the strongest English mustard

Pork and sage

The finest Ratbridge Old Spot pork combined with a compound
formed of four-fifths fresh sage, one-tenth ground cloves,
one tenth ground black pepper

Venison and redcurrant jelly

A combination of venison with a precisely-set jelly
formulated from 19 redcurrants per pie

Rhubarb and ginger

An amalgam of rhubarb and ginger, with one third of an ounce of cardamom,
and heated for 47 minutes to a temperate 108 degrees centigrade

All pie vessels are formed from pastry which has been made from flour
specially milled to a density of thirty-six pounds per cubic foot.

Madame Froufrou

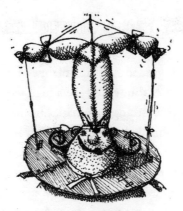

A very strange woman

Chapter 13

MADAME FROUFROU

Arthur and Willbury set off across the market in the direction of the Patent Hall, Arthur trying to keep up with Willbury as they pushed their way through the crowds again. As they reached the edge of the market the crowds became even denser until finally they could no longer find their way through, and were forced to come to a stop.

They were in the middle of a large crowd of ladies, all of whom seemed in a state of high excitement. It was clear there was something unusual going on.

'What do you think is happening?' Arthur had to raise his voice to make himself heard above the sound of chattering and twittering.

'I am not sure. There seems to be a platform with someone on,' Willbury called back.

Willbury then guided Arthur in front of him. The crowd parted a little and Arthur could see a high wooden platform. On it stood a very strange woman. She wore a dress that looked as if it was made from skinned sofa and cardboard, an enormous pink wig, and a pair of rubber gauntlets. She also had a patch over one eye.

'Who is it?' asked Arthur. Despite never having seen a woman dressed in such a way before, Arthur felt the woman was oddly familiar, but for the life of him, he didn't know where from.

The woman standing next to them overheard Arthur's question. 'Don't you know? It's Madame Froufrou . . . the fashion princess!'

Willbury and Arthur looked at each other, shrugged their shoulders, and turned back to watch.

The strange woman raised her arms to quiet the crowd and the din died down. The ladies of the town were now all aquiver, and some let out squeals of delight.

'What has she got this week?' one whispered.

'I heard it's something really special . . . and totally new,' replied another.

'I can hardly bear it,' said the first. 'I missed out last week and they haven't let me in the tearooms since.'

The woman on the platform glowered at the crowd. A silence fell, but was broken by the sound of a large wooden box being slid up onto the stage. The woman started to speak.

'Today, my little fashion friends, Madame Froufrou 'as a real treat for you.'

Little cries of 'Magnifique!' 'Wunderbar!' 'I must have one' 'I must have two', came from the crowd.

The lady on the platform gave a smirk. She leaned over to the box, opened a door in its lid, and reached in with her large rubber-gloved hand. She paused, then looked about the crowd, and gave them what was supposed to be a look of delight. Then slowly she pulled out a tiny creature. It was a miniature boxtroll.

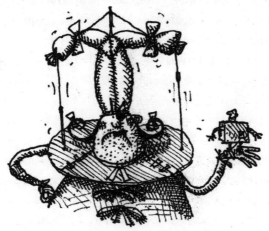

Then slowly she pulled out a tiny creature

The crowd let out a gasp of admiration. Arthur turned to Willbury. They both looked shocked.

'It's just like the ones Gristle brought to the shop! What do you think is going on?' asked Arthur.

'I am not sure, but I don't like it!' replied Willbury. 'Let's watch.'

Madame Froufrou started to speak again. ''Ere I 'ave a lickle lap creature, just the very sort the finest ladies of Pari are clamouring for as we speak. I 'ave a very limited supply and I'm afraid that some 'ere will be left in a sad and lonely fashion backwater.'

She paused and stared at the crowd. A soft pitiful moaning started from all around Arthur and Willbury.

'I cannot 'elp this, but it is for you to decide whether you are a woman of tomorrow or merely a ugly frump . . . with no sense of taste . . . or chance of social position!'

At this the ladies of the town started a desperate squeaking.

Then someone cried: 'Me, me, sell one to me!'

Others immediately joined in the cry. 'ME, ME, Me, No! Me, ME!'

The noise grew so loud that Arthur had to put down his shopping and put his hands over his ears.

Madame Froufrou raised a hand. The cries halted and all that could be heard was the snapping of opening purses, and coins being counted.

'I cannot be kind to you all . . . My supplies are very limited.'

Someone in the audience let out a miserable whimper.

'Should Madame Froufrou choose the ladies at the front to give the opportunity to buy these sweet treasures?'

Cries of 'No! No! No!' came from the back of the crowd.

A fashionable lady of Pari

'Should I choose only those who are wearing this week's pink?' asked Madame Froufrou, grinning.

'No! No! No!' came the cries from all but those who wore pink.

'I think I shall do as they do in Pari,' said Madame Froufrou.

'Yes! Yes! Yes!' cried the ladies. 'Do what they do in Pari!'

'Yes, I shall do what they do in Pari. I shall do what is the latest thing . . . and select only from those who are . . . fashionably . . . RICH!' Madame Froufrou came to a halt and several ladies in the crowd fainted.

She scanned the crowd. 'Now, there is a question you must ask yourselves. Am I fashionably RICH? If you are not . . . you must cast yourself from this world of glamour and

retire to your true miserable and rightfully low position.'
She glowered at the crowd.

There was silence for a moment then cries of 'I am rich! I
am rich! I am rich!' came from the ladies around Arthur and
Willbury.

Again Madame Froufrou raised her hand and silence
returned.

'What a joy it is to be in such fashionable company.
But . . . I have a feeling that hiding amongst us are some . . .
DOWDY FRUMPS!'

A dowdy frump

Arthur noticed that the women around him all started to
tremble with fear.

Madame Froufrou paused a long time for dramatic effect,
then spoke again. 'I shall have to weed them out . . .

BUT HOW?' There was another very long pause as she peered around the crowd. 'I have an idea . . . an idea that will show up the dowdy frumps hiding amongst us!'

Several more ladies in the crowd fainted.

Madame Froufrou started again. 'Could the fashionable ladies here please raise their hands and display the most fashionable quantities of money they can . . . And please do check that those around you are fashionable!'

Hundreds of hands shot up and started to wave money

For a few moments all that could be heard was the rustling of banknotes and clinking of coins. Then hundreds of hands shot up and started to wave money. The ladies looked nervously around. Madame Froufrou now took out an enormous pair of binoculars and started to scan the crowd.

'As I look at you all, I am shocked that one whole area is obviously harbouring the dowdy trying to pass themselves off as fashionable . . . '

Nervous twitching broke out.

'I shall turn my back for a moment and let them crawl away . . . for if they are still here when I turn back . . . I shall

POINT THEM OUT!' With that she turned her back.

The ladies now struggled to find every last penny to hold up in an attempt to avoid being labelled a frump.

Madame Froufrou turned slowly back and smiled. 'Ah! I see they have fled! It is only the stylish that remain.'

'Yes! Yes!' cried the crowd in relief.

'Well, it is time for us to impart the new and ultimate accessory upon those who deserve it! Come hither, Roberto and Raymond.'

Two men dressed in dirty pink suits climbed onto the stage.

'These are my French fashion specialists and they are here to help me select those who are the most fashionable. Roberto and Raymond, please take out your fashion scopes and wands . . . Divine those that are expectable!'

Two men dressed in dirty pink suits climbed onto the stage

Roberto and Raymond pulled out what looked like binoculars made from toilet rolls, and fishing rods with small buckets hung on the end. Looking through their binoculars they started to scan the crowd.

Looking through their binoculars they started to scan the crowd

Roberto's gaze fixed upon a particularly full hand and he turned to Madame Froufrou. 'Madame, I think I see a fashion angel,' he said, indicating the 'angel' in the crowd.

'Yes, it is true! A woman of grace and virtue! Now my angel, if you would place your offering in the bucket affixed to our fashion wand, and take a numbered ticket, I shall invite you to collect your very precious new lifestyle accessory from the stage, and lo . . . You shall be a queen amongst women!'

Roberto took out a grubby ticket from his pocket and put it in the bucket at the end of his wand. Then he swung the wand out over the crowd to the angel's outstretched arm. The woman pushed all of her money into the bucket, took the ticket, and squeaked as she made her way towards the stage. Looks of hatred and envy followed her. The bucket swung back over the crowd and disappeared. When the angel had made her way to the stage Madame Froufrou passed the tiny boxtroll down to her in exchange for the ticket.

Madame Froufrou passed the tiny boxtroll down to her in exchange for the ticket

Roberto and Raymond began selecting more members of the crowd and exchanging tickets for cash, while Madame Froufrou stood by the wooden box and collected the tickets, and handed out more miniature boxtrolls. The crowd of ladies rapidly thinned, as they handed over their cash, collected their new pets, and set off in small groups to parade them.

Then Arthur and Willbury watched as Madame Froufrou turned to what remained of the crowd.

There were now only three ladies, Willbury, and Arthur left. The remaining women still held their handfuls of cash aloft, as they quietly wept.

Madame Froufrou saw Arthur and for a moment fixed him with a rather steely gaze, before turning her eye on the ladies.

'Do you know her?' whispered Willbury.

'I am not sure, but there is something about her. I get the feeling that I have met her before,' Arthur muttered nervously.

'And from the look of it, I think she thinks she knows you!' Willbury replied.

Madame Froufrou was now asking Roberto and Raymond some questions. They answered and she turned back to her remaining customers.

'We have I am afraid sold out of our little friends in the box, but it is not my way to let you POOR ladies go home with no chance of social position. It seems I have a late special offer.'

The remaining ladies let out their breath. Roberto and Raymond disappeared down behind the stage and after a few moments three large zinc buckets were passed up.

Arthur stared at the buckets, then turned to Willbury. 'You're not thinking what I am thinking about those buckets, are you?'

Willbury was looking shocked. 'If I am, this is definitely more than a coincidence!'

'Come closer, ladies. In these vessels are some very special creatures that have only come into fashion in the last few minutes . . . ' Madame Froufrou whispered.

The remaining ladies suddenly started to look happy again as they made their way to the front of the stage.

'Yes! The very, very latest. Fresh-water sea-cows! Dredged from the banks of the Seine. These creatures are the very height of chic in the bathrooms of Pari and Milan.'

The ladies started to giggle, and Willbury picked up his shopping. 'Quick, Arthur. Grab your things. I am going to have words with this Madame Froufrou.'

Arthur picked up the sack and shopping bag, and followed Willbury towards the platform.

'Excuse me, madam!' called Willbury. Madame Froufrou looked up at Willbury, then down at the ladies, then back at the approaching Willbury.

'I am sorry, ladies, but I have to go.' She snatched the money from the outstretched hands. 'Help yourselves to the buckets.' Then she turned and jumped off the back of the stage.

'Excuse me, madam! Where do you think you are going?' shouted Willbury. 'I want words with you!'

Arthur followed Willbury as he ran round to the back of the platform.

Madame Froufrou and her assistants were gone.

After a few moments Willbury spoke. 'You said she looked familiar. Do you know where you might have seen her?'

'I'm not sure where I could have seen her before. I know it's strange, but I got the same feeling when I was looking at her, that I got when the leader of the cheese hunt cornered me. She could have been his twin sister.'

'Very strange . . . ' Willbury paused to think. 'Something is very wrong . . . And weird. I think we had better go and find Marjorie. Maybe she can throw some light on things.'

Madame Froufrou and her assistants were gone

Outside the Patent Hall

A miniature French poodle

Chapter 14

THE PATENT HALL

Willbury and Arthur made their way up the side streets towards the Patent Hall, and as they went they talked.

'Before today I'd never seen, nor even heard of, miniature boxtrolls, cabbageheads, sea-cows, or trotting badgers. And now miniatures seem to be everywhere. It's very odd,' said Willbury.

'I suppose there are different types of creature in different countries,' said Arthur.

'True. I've heard of miniature French poodles, so I guess France might be the home of a lot of small things,' added Willbury. 'But I don't like something about what's going on. Think how unhappy those poor creatures were when they arrived at the shop . . . And as for Madame Froufrou . . . Well! The less said about her the better!'

'I just don't understand what is going on,' said Arthur. He felt bewildered and rather sad.

'Yes, it is all rather odd,' replied Willbury. Then he paused for a moment as he thought. 'This business of the hunt leader and Madame Froufrou looking like brother and sister is strange. I wonder if all this bother is tied up in some way?'

'Do you think your friend Marjorie might be able to help?' asked Arthur.

'I do hope so,' replied Willbury. 'She might not be able to shed any light on this matter of the miniature creatures, but I suppose we should concentrate on our own problems at the moment. Getting you back to your grandfather, and getting your wings back. As I said, Marjorie knows pretty well everybody who has anything to do with mechanics in the town. I am hoping that she will help us track down your wings.'

'Who is Marjorie?' asked Arthur.

'Marjorie was my clerk. Very bright woman. She used to deal with patent claims mostly. Invariably she could understand most inventions better than their creators, so when I retired she decided to go into inventing, rather than sticking with law. She has a natural aptitude for it. A lot of the legal stuff can be very boring so I was not surprised. Anyway, with all the legal work she did with patents and now with her own inventing, she knows everybody who has anything to do with machines and the like. Though it is quite a secretive world, if you are trusted like she is, you do get to hear what is going on.'

'Marjorie was my clerk'

'So do you suppose she might hear where my wings are?'

'That is what I was hoping, but even supposing we do get your wings back, we still have to get you back underground.' Willbury looked sad.

'Yes . . . I have been thinking about Grandfather . . . ' Arthur's voice trailed off.

Willbury put a hand on Arthur's shoulder to comfort him. 'There have to be other ways to get you back into the Underworld.'

'There are,' said Arthur. 'But I just don't know where!'

Willbury stopped in his tracks. 'What do you mean? Have you heard of other routes to the underground?'

'Yes,' said Arthur.

'Arthur, this could be very important. Tell me everything!'

'Well, lots of creatures live underground, and not just under Ratbridge . . . A lot of their tunnels are linked up. It might be possible to get down one of the tunnels outside Ratbridge, and get back to Grandfather. But I just don't know where the other tunnels come out above ground . . .

And it might be dangerous,' Arthur replied.

'Dangerous?' Willbury sounded surprised.

'Yes. I was always warned to stay away from the outer tunnels. Trotting badgers live in some of them . . . and they can be very, very nasty. Grandfather lost a finger to one when he was younger.'

A trotting badger

'Are trotting badgers the only creatures that have tunnels outside the town?' asked Willbury.

'No. There are rabbits . . . and rabbit women.'

'Rabbit women? I thought they were just a myth.'

'No! They exist. I saw them once when I was exploring . . . well, not actually them . . . I found a home cave,' replied Arthur.

'Home cave?'

'It's a place where they live. You can tell it's a home cave by the things they leave about—scraps of food, ash, rabbit droppings, and suits the rabbit women have knitted from rabbit wool.'

'So do you know where the rabbit women's holes are? Could we find one?' asked Willbury.

A rabbit woman knitting rabbit wool

'No.' Arthur looked very sad. 'I don't think so. They are very, very secretive, and keep themselves very much to themselves. They have to . . . to avoid the trotting badgers.' He paused. 'Besides, the rabbit women are so good at tunnelling that their holes could be miles away.'

It had started to drizzle. They both felt glum and fell silent as they walked. Soon they came to a small cross roads and Willbury pointed down one of the streets.

'This way. The Patent Hall is not far now.'

'By the way, what is a patent?' asked Arthur.

'Oh! That was my speciality as a lawyer.' Willbury perked up a little. 'A patent is a legal certificate given by the government to the inventor of some new device or idea or process. The patent says that because it is their idea they are the owner of that invention. This gives them the right to use their invention without others copying it without their permission. The patent will last for some years and that way the inventor can profit from their invention.'

'Does that mean that if I had invented string, I could charge everybody who made or sold string?'

'Yes, Arthur, if you had invented string you would be a very, very rich man.' Willbury chuckled.

'So what happens at the Patent Hall?'

'It's a government office where inventors go to get patents. They have to prove that their ideas work and are totally new.'

They turned up another side street and there in front of them stood the Patent Hall. It was a fine building with a frontage that looked like a Greek temple. Arthur had noticed it before when he had been flying, but approaching it on foot it seemed far bigger than he remembered. There was a queue of inventors that started in the street, led up the steps, past the pillared entrance, and disappeared through a huge pair of oak doors. The members of the queue all carried carefully

wrapped bundles and looked round nervously at Arthur and Willbury as they passed by.

'Why are they looking at us like that?' asked Arthur.

'They are all worried that someone might steal their ideas before they are registered and patented,' said Willbury. 'There are people that come here specially to try and get their hands on new ideas, and rob the poor inventors of their patents.'

Willbury led Arthur up the steps of the Patent Hall, and in through the doors. Just inside was a desk where a man was handing out tickets to people in the queue. Beyond was a large crowded hall. Down either side of the hall was a series of tents, each with a number on. The tents were made of thick canvas that had seen better days and was now covered in burns and a multitude of stains. Strange noises, and the odd flash of light, came from several of the tents. Outside each of these tents stood a queue of even more nervous-looking inventors.

'That is where the inventors give the initial demonstrations. If they get through that they are sent upstairs to have their inventions checked for originality,' said Willbury.

At the far end of the hall was a large staircase and by it stood a group of very shifty-looking men. Arthur caught Willbury giving them a very suspicious glance.

'Failed Patent Acquisition Officers! Scum!' Arthur was shocked by Willbury's mutterings.

'Who is?' asked Arthur.

'That lot at the foot of the stairs!' Willbury pointed an accusing finger. 'They are the very scum of the mechanical world. Technical vultures! They hit a man when he's down, and by the time he recovers they have either made off with his invention or have him so tied up in contracts that he either has to buy them off or hand the whole thing over to them. Vermin! They should be locked up!'

'How do they do that?' asked Arthur.

'Well, if an inventor isn't granted a patent because his idea is not fully developed or the patent officers just don't understand it, the inventor can get very upset and disheartened . . . and that lot . . . ' Willbury pointed his finger again at the group at the bottom of the stairs. ' . . . that lot . . . move in on him.'

The Failed Patent Acquisition Officers had spotted Willbury pointing at them, and were now trying either to hide behind the tents or slide along the walls and out of the entrance.

Willbury's voice grew louder. 'Every day they assemble there at the bottom of the stairs, waiting for their chance to spring . . . They watch for unhappy faces leaving the tents,

The very scum of the mechanical world

then . . . with all the slime they can muster they approach the man and offer him "sympathy"! They might take him round the corner for a cup of tea, offer him a biscuit or piece of cake, tell him they might have a few bob to help him out and take his project further, ask him to just sign a little document to show they are pals and will be willing to have fun together . . . and before he knows what's hit him he doesn't own the clothes he stands up in! The scum then turn the screw. They make the man finish his project under the threat of legal action, then sell it on once it's patented . . . without a single penny going back to the inventor.'

Willbury's voice could now be heard throughout the hall. He took a turnip from his shopping bag and threw it at the last of the Failed Patent Acquisition Officers, who was disappearing out of the main doors.

There was a yelp from outside, and some of the older inventors cheered.

He took a turnip from his shopping bag and threw it

'Very satisfactory!' said Willbury, rubbing his hands. 'When I was a lawyer it was a favourite pastime of mine to break the grasp of those filth. I have very happily kicked their posteriors on a number of occasions! And if there was one thing that would persuade me to come out of retirement it would be the opportunity to kick a few more.'

Arthur looked a little startled.

'Now,' said Willbury, 'let us find Marjorie!'

Willbury looked around the hall, walked over to one of the queues, and asked, 'Does anybody know where Marjorie is?'

Several arms pointed up to the balcony on the first floor. Arthur and Willbury set off up the stairs. When they reached the top Willbury led Arthur to a small desk at the far end of the balcony. A small tent was erected by the side of the desk, and outside it in a deckchair sat a very unhappy looking woman, reading a book of mathematical tables. Willbury coughed and the woman looked up.

A small tent was erected by the side of the desk, and outside
it in a deck chair sat a very unhappy looking woman

'Good morning, Marjorie,' said Willbury. 'I would like you to meet a good friend of mine: Arthur. How are you?'

The woman dropped the book of tables to her lap, then spoke. 'Not well, Mr Nibble. Not well. I have been stuck here for months . . . and things are not looking good!' She paused for a moment, then stood up and reached out a hand to Arthur. 'I am sorry. It is very impolite of me. I am pleased to meet you, Arthur. It's just everything has gone wrong for me.'

Arthur took her hand, shook it, and gave her a sympathetic smile.

'I did come here to ask you for some help, but before we

get onto that can you tell me what has happened to you?' asked Willbury.

'I came here three months ago with my new invention, did my initial demonstration downstairs, and then was sent up here to see a Mr Edward Trout. He had to check the machine for originality. I was a bit dubious when he said he was taking it away for inspection. Then he didn't come back!'

'What! He disappeared?' asked Willbury.

'Yes! That's right. I can prove that I gave him a machine because I've got a receipt, but because my receipt has no description of my machine on it, I can't prove what it is that they have got of mine. They keep trying to get rid of me by sending out junior clerks with any old rubbish they can find in the warehouse! But I won't leave until they give me back my invention!'

'Oh dear, dear me!' said Willbury. 'This is terrible. How have you managed to survive?'

'Yes, it is terrible, but the other inventors have been very good about it. They have brought me food when they can . . . and this tent and chair. I have just about got enough to live on, but I can't spend the rest of my life here.'

The receipt

A junior clerk with a piece of rubbish from the warehouse

Willbury looked very concerned. 'No . . . no, you can't.'

Marjorie spoke again. 'The clerk who disappeared has apparently now left the employment of the patent office, and I am very scared that he just ran off with my invention.'

'Ran off with your invention? What was it?' asked Willbury.

Marjorie looked around furtively, then she whispered to Willbury, 'I know I can trust you Mr Nibble . . . but at this point I think it better that no one knows!'

'Oh!' said Willbury. 'If you are sure. Is it the sort of invention that others might want to steal?'

'Yes! Mr Nibble, it is fantastic,' Marjorie whispered. 'It is the culmination of the last two years' work . . . But in the wrong hands it could be very dangerous . . . and now it has either been stolen, or lost!' Marjorie was looking very upset, and Willbury took her hand in his.

Arthur caught Willbury's eye, and pointed to the sack.

'You will never get in to see him Mr Nibble!'

'I know it may be of little comfort, but we have brought you some pies from Mr Whitworth,' said Willbury. 'Arthur, could you get them out while I go and have a word with the Head Patent Officer, Mr Louis Trout.'

'Louis Trout?' said Marjorie. 'It was an Edward Trout that went off with my machine.'

'I had heard that Louis Trout's son had joined the office. It must have been him,' said Willbury. 'I am sure that he will know exactly what has happened.'

'You will never get in to see him, Mr Nibble!' said Marjorie. 'I have been trying for weeks.'

'I think I shall! He knows me from a certain legal case . . . and if I let one or two things drop in conversation with his receptionist I think he will see me very quickly.'

With that Willbury left Arthur and Marjorie, and disappeared into the grandest of the doors along the balcony.

Marjorie's eye fixed on the sack. 'Err . . . um. What flavour pies are they?'

'We've got six pork and sage, a couple of turkey and ham, and Mr Whitworth gave me a cake as well. You can share that with me if you want?' offered Arthur.

Suddenly Marjorie looked a lot more perky. 'It's not one of Mr Whitworth's mulberry cakes, is it?'

'I am not sure,' replied Arthur. 'Why?'

'You wouldn't be offering to share it if it was,' Marjorie jested.

Arthur reached inside the sack and pulled out the smallest of the bundles, then unwrapped it. The cake was pink and dotted with small pieces of fruit.

'It is!' declared Marjorie. 'Joy upon joy. Do you really not mind sharing it?'

Arthur grinned. 'I don't mind.' And he broke the cake in two and passed half to Marjorie. She stared at the cake and after a few moments closed her eyes and took a bit of it. Arthur watched her, then did the same. As soon as the cake entered his mouth the flavour burst over his tongue. Marjorie was right—it was a joy. He opened his eyes to see Marjorie stuff the rest of her half of the cake into her mouth at one go.

'You must be very hungry?' asked Arthur. Marjorie nodded, then after a deep swallow spoke again.

'Now I remember food! My stomach thought that my throat had been cut. Do you mind if I get stuck into a pork and sage pie . . . or two?'

Arthur reached inside the sack again and pulled out the

rest of the parcels. He unwrapped one and noticed it had a pig made of pastry stuck on the top.

'I guess this must be pork and sage then?'

'Yes. Mr Whitworth always puts a sign on his pies so you can recognize what's inside.' Arthur passed her the pie. 'I have to thank you for bringing these to me. It is very kind.'

Something occurred to Arthur. This was the first woman he had ever spoken to and he felt a little bashful. He watched as Marjorie tucked into the pie, then there was a noise from along the balcony. Willbury had reappeared and was looking very flushed and angry.

'What's the matter, Willbury?' asked Arthur.

'Pack up your things, Marjorie! The Head Patent Officer, Mr Louis Trout, has taken early retirement and gone off to set up a new business with his son . . . the man who disappeared with your invention!'

Marjorie lowered the pie from her mouth, swallowed, then spoke. 'They've stolen my machine!'

'I am sorry but it looks as if it might well be that way,' said Willbury.

'What do I do?' asked Marjorie. 'Do I stay here and wait for ever, or do I go in search of the Trouts . . . and for ever lose my chance of recovering my invention here?'

Willbury spoke in a soft voice. 'I think the chances of getting your machine back here at the moment are almost nil. Your last chance is to file an official complaint . . . Come with us now and I will help you draft one. And besides,

'What do I do?' asked Marjorie

I think we need your help. If you come with us I'll explain why.'

They collected up their things and then they set off back across the town to the shop. Marjorie was muttering about what she might do if she ever caught up with the Trouts, Arthur was worrying about Grandfather and his wings, and Willbury had a face like thunder. And then things got worse . . .

Willbury, Arthur, and Marjorie stood in the doorway of the shop and just stared

Even Willbury's armchair had been broken and upended

Chapter 15

GONE!

Willbury, Arthur, and Marjorie stood in the doorway of the shop and just stared. The door had been broken from its hinges, and inside the comfortable untidiness had been reduced to a broken shambles.

'Oh no!' Willbury whispered under his breath. 'What's happened?'

Arthur felt shocked, and a little afraid. He reached up and took Willbury's hand. The room was a pitiful sight. The bookcases were overturned, the curtains torn, and newspapers and books were scattered over the floor. Even Willbury's armchair had been broken and upended.

Arthur felt Willbury's grasp suddenly grow tight. Willbury cleared his throat then called out. 'Fish! Titus! Egg! Shoe! Where are you?' He was met with silence. He spoke again but this time there was real worry in his voice. 'Where are the creatures?'

Arthur broke free of Willbury's grip and ran across the room to look behind the counter, then he ran out through the door to the back room and hall. He returned looking very glum. 'They're not here.'

Willbury walked forward into the centre of the shop, and stopped. He reached down and picked up a torn piece of cardboard, raised it to his nose, and sniffed.

He raised the torn piece of cardboard to his nose and sniffed

'Fish!' he muttered, and clutched the piece of cardboard to his chest.

Arthur walked forward to Willbury. Willbury looked down at Arthur. 'Something awful has happened!'

Suddenly Arthur noticed that his feet felt cold. He looked down and realized that he was standing on a piece of sodden carpet. There by his feet was the fish tank on its side. He leaned down. In the shadow of the earthenware jar lay the miniature sea-cow. It didn't move, and Arthur was not sure if it was still alive. Willbury followed Arthur's gaze and dropped to his knees.

'Quick, Arthur, fetch a jug full of water!'

Arthur ran out to the back of the shop, found a jug, filled it, and rushed back. Willbury slowly righted the tank as he filled it from the jug. The sea-cow floated on the surface of the water. They all stared at her body, hoping they were not too late. After a few moments it twitched and started to move.

'Thank God!' said Willbury. 'I hope it's going to be all right. Arthur, go and get more water.' He gently lifted the tank and placed it back on the counter. Arthur refilled the jug, and soon the tank was full.

Willbury slowly righted the tank as he filled it from the jug

'Where do you think everyone is?' asked Arthur.

'I am not sure . . . ' said Willbury as he looked about. He lifted a bookshelf upright and started to place a few books back on it. Marjorie joined him.

'What shall I do?' asked Arthur.

'Would you see to that water?' Willbury pointed at the damp patch on the carpet. 'Collect up some newspapers, and use them to soak it up.'

Arthur walked towards some newspapers that lay strewn across the floor. Lifting a handful of them, he suddenly let out a gasp. There, huddled on the floor, shaking uncontrollably, was the miniature boxtroll.

'It's Match!' cried Arthur to Willbury.

The tiny boxtroll ran straight at Arthur and threw its arms around his ankle. Arthur looked down at Match, and something shiny on the carpet caught his eye. It was Match's nut and bolt. Arthur reached down and gently picked up Match, then with his other hand picked up the nut and bolt and passed it to Match's outstretched arms. Match took the nut and bolt and snuggled into Arthur.

The tiny boxtroll threw its arms around Arthur's ankle

'That's right. You take care of Match,' said Willbury.

Marjorie looked at the miniature boxtroll, then walked over and looked in the tank. She did not say a word but looked very uneasy.

'What is it, Marjorie?' asked Willbury.

'Nothing.' Marjorie paused. 'Where did these tiny creatures come from?'

'I bought them this morning from an awful man called Gristle . . . ' Willbury stopped. 'He wanted to buy Fish . . . and the other big creatures. He was desperate to get his hands on them. I wonder if he was behind this? If so, he is going to pay for it!'

'We saw miniature creatures today at the market, too,' Arthur said. 'Willbury, do you think that Gristle has something to do with Madame Froufrou?'

'I am not sure, but whatever is going on, we have got to get Fish and the others back!' declared Willbury. 'I don't know why Gristle wanted them, but I can't help feeling they're in terrible danger.' He looked around the room again and his eyes fixed on the barrel in the corner. 'Titus!' he exclaimed and rushed to the barrel. Willbury got down on his knees and peered through the hole in the side.

'Oh dear, you poor thing!' said Willbury. He reached inside the barrel and pulled the tiny cabbagehead out. 'Titus may be gone . . . but his little friend is still with us.'

Willbury held the miniature cabbagehead in his hand and gently stroked it. It too was shaking.

Willbury held the miniature cabbagehead in his hand and gently stroked it

'Poor thing,' Willbury said mournfully.

As Willbury, Arthur, and Marjorie were fussing over the tiny cabbagehead, thinking about how to comfort him, there was a sudden coughing from the shop doorway. They spun round, fearful of who they would see there. But the sight that greeted them was quite unexpected—it appeared to be a large basket full of dirty washing supported by a pair of legs.

A large basket full of dirty washing supported by a pair of legs

'Good morning! Need any washing done?' The washing lowered itself to the floor, and from behind it stepped a smiling man with a platform made of sticks fixed to his head. On the platform sat a large and friendly-looking rat, wearing a spotted handkerchief tied around his head.

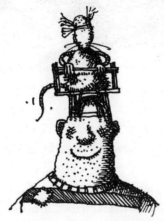

On the platform sat a large and friendly-looking rat

'This is Kipper,' the rat said, indicating the man below, 'and my name is Tom. Business card, please, Kipper!'

The man with the platform fixed on his head pulled out a tiny business card from his pocket, passed it to the rat, who then held it out. Willbury walked forward, took the card and read it.

First Mate Tom R.N.L.
The Ratbridge Nautical Laundry
We wash whiter and boil things brighter
No load too big or filthy

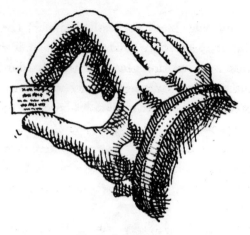

The tiny business card

Willbury was not sure whether to address the rat or the man beneath.

'It's all right,' said the man called Kipper. 'I'm just the muscle round here. You deal with the boss.'

'Boss?' cried the rat. 'Not boss! This is a working co-operative. We are all equal in the Ratbridge Nautical Laundry. It is true that I deal with the customer interface, and you deal with the load management. But you know that last week when we tried it the other way round . . . it all went horribly wrong!'

'True enough, Tom. You're rubbish at shifting things and I am rubbish at organizing stuff. Anyway, sir,' Kipper said turning to Willbury, 'if you would like to deal with Tom here, as he is the brains of this outfit, I shall just stand beneath until required.'

'Yes,' said Tom the rat. 'Now, may we be of any service to you? You are very lucky as this week is our "Big Smalls Promotion". As we are new in this area, the Ratbridge Nautical Laundry is offering a special introductory offer to new customers. As much underwear as you like boil washed, free . . . if you get two shirts and a pair of trousers . . . '

Tom stopped. Kipper had just poked him in the ribs.

'I think our friends here have got more on their minds than cheap deals on getting their underwear washed,' said Kipper.

Tom looked at Willbury, Arthur, and Marjorie, then about the shop.

'Oh, my Gawd! What's happened here? Closing down sale?' he asked.

'No, I think we have been raided and our friends snatched,' replied Willbury.

'Oh!' said Tom. 'Please excuse my patter.' He looked genuinely concerned. 'When did this happen?'

'In the last hour or so. We've just got back from town, and this is what we found on our return,' said Willbury.

'Did you say your friends are missing?' asked Kipper.

Willbury looked slowly about the room. 'Yes, our dear, dear friends are missing.'

'How many were there?' asked Tom.

'Four—Fish, Shoe, Egg, and Titus,' said Arthur.

'They're three boxtrolls . . . and a cabbagehead,' added Willbury.

'Boxtrolls and cabbageheads?' asked Tom. 'What, like those creatures?'

Tom pointed to Match, who Arthur was still holding, and to the tiny cabbagehead that Willbury was trying to comfort.

'Yes,' said Willbury. 'Only much, much bigger.'

'Oh dear!' said Tom. 'How terrible!'

Then Kipper spoke. 'We've had three of our crew disappear in the last couple of weeks . . . '

'What?' cried Willbury. 'This has happened to you as well?'

'Yes. When the first one disappeared we thought he might have just run away, but last week two more disappeared, and we're sure that something bad has happened to them . . . The last two were good mates . . . not the type to run off,' said Kipper.

The first to go was a very unpopular rat called Framley

'What happened?' asked Arthur. 'Did you have a break-in like this?'

'The first to go was a very unpopular rat called Framley. He was a nasty piece of work so nobody was sorry to see the back of him. He just disappeared one day from the laundry,' said Kipper.

'That Framley . . . If he hadn't gone I think he would have been booted out, anyway,' added Tom. 'We were all a little wary of him, to be honest—felt he could turn violent at any time. But then last week we lost two more rats. This time it was Pickles and Levi. They were really good blokes. Disappeared on a shopping trip.'

'This is very peculiar!' said Willbury. 'Have you got any idea where they might have gone?'

'I think you should talk to the captain,' said Tom. 'He's started an investigation. Why don't you come back with us to the ship?'

Kipper looked up at Tom, and Tom corrected himself. 'Erm . . . laundry?'

'Well . . . ' Willbury looked around the shop. 'I hate to leave the shop like this. But if you think your captain might be able to help us get our friends back, then of course that's more important than this mess.'

'Don't worry about clearing this place up. We can send a party from the laundry to tidy up for you,' said Kipper.

'That is very kind of you, but . . . ' said Willbury.

'Not at all. We insist!' replied Kipper. 'The crew really

enjoy tidying things up and cleaning. It's all those years at sea.'

'Well, thank you,' said Willbury. 'Do you mind if we go and talk to your captain right now? We need to get to the bottom of this as quickly as possible.'

'Certainly! Follow us,' replied Tom. 'Up Kipper and home! And don't spare the horses!'

Kipper took up the huge laundry basket and pulled its straps over his shoulders.

Arthur turned to Willbury. 'What about Match, the sea-cow, and Titus's little friend?'

'Take them with us. We can't leave them here.' Willbury slipped the tiny cabbagehead into the top pocket of his jacket.

'Marjorie. Do you think you could put the sea-cow back in the bucket with some water? We can't leave her alone.'

'Certainly,' said Marjorie. She took the bucket the sea-cow had arrived in, and after a bit of gentle fussing, she managed to get her out of the tank and into the bucket with some water.

Off they set to the laundry. As they walked, Arthur held Match tight to him and talked to him in a gentle voice.

'Don't worry, Match, we'll get the others back. It's all going to be all right.'

Match seemed comforted by Arthur's words, but Arthur wondered to himself if they were true.

The Ratbridge Nautical Laundry

The pink and white ensign flown when washing is on the boil

Chapter 16

PANTS AHOY!

The canal ran along the backs of factories. Once it had been Ratbridge's main commercial link with the outer world. Barges had brought coal and other raw materials to the town, and had taken goods manufactured there out to the world. The canal had bustled with life. But since the coming of the steam railway, it had not been much used, except by unambitious fishermen, and small boys with model boats. Then a few weeks ago a large ship had somehow lodged itself under the canal bridge, and as its crew needed an income, and because of their limited skills, they had 'launched' the Ratbridge Nautical Laundry. The crew was unusual in that it consisted of a mixture of sailors and rats, working as equal partners together. Rumour had it that they had a long and interesting history, and that before they turned their hands to laundry they had been an altogether less respectable crew, but nobody in Ratbridge knew that much about them yet.

Rain was just starting to fall as the little group led by Kipper and Tom turned onto the towpath. Ahead of them was a very peculiar sight. The aft of the wooden sailing ship filled the canal. Steam rose from a tall chimney positioned on the main deck, and wafted through what looked like ragged sails that were fluttering from the rigging. As they drew closer they could hear a rhythmical hissing and throbbing of machinery. Arthur felt Match twitching. He looked down and saw that Match was becoming very excited.

'What is it, Match?' The miniature boxtroll pointed towards the steam and squeaked.

There was something large and green moving slowly up and down amongst the steam.

'You've got a beam engine!' exclaimed Marjorie, almost dropping the bucket with the fresh-water sea-cow in.

Kipper turned back and smiled. 'Yes. It's a really big one!'

'Where did you get it from?' Marjorie sounded excited.

Kipper looked a little nervous, and Tom spoke. 'Er . . . We acquired it . . . on a recent trip to Cornwall . . . '

'How do you acquire a beam engine?' asked Marjorie.

'With a great deal of pushing and shoving . . . ' replied Kipper.

'Can't say much, but it was superfluous to the needs of its owners,' said Tom.

'And we won't be going back there on holiday any time soon,' Kipper added. Tom looked a bit shifty. Willbury gave them a rather suspicious look.

'What's a beam engine?' Arthur asked.

'It's a sort of steam engine, but it usually stays fixed in one place. Instead of moving things like a railway engine, it uses its power to work machines,' Marjorie explained. Her eyes were shining. 'It's a most incredible invention.'

They were approaching the gangplank that ran from the towpath onto the deck of the ship. Arthur looked up and realized the 'sails' were in fact hundreds of pieces of washing, pegged onto the rigging and flapping in the breeze.

'All aboard!' cried Kipper, and the little group made their way up onto the deck of the Ratbridge Nautical Laundry. Sitting on the rails that ran down both sides of the deck sat some twenty miserable-looking crows.

'What's up, Mildred?' asked Tom.

'Rain!' answered one of the crows. 'We just got this load hung out when it started.'

'Aren't you going to take it in?' asked Tom.

'Doesn't seem much point as it is already wet,' said Mildred. 'Besides, where are we going to put it? The hold is full of dirty washing, the bilges have got another load in, and the crew quarters are packed with boxes of washing powder.'

Miserable-looking crows

Tom turned to Willbury, Arthur, and Marjorie. 'I'll take you down below to try and find the captain, but first we need to check in this washing. Kipper . . . the hatch!'

Kipper walked to a large hatch set in the deck, and put the basket down. Then he stamped three times on the deck, and the hatch opened. A friendly-looking rat jumped out, and spoke.

'Morning, Kipper! Morning, Tom! Got the list to go with this lot?' he asked as he pointed to the washing in the basket. Kipper produced a long strip of paper, and handed it to the rat.

'Can you be very careful with the big woolly underpants, Jim?' said Tom. 'I know that wool has a tendency to shrink, and the lady who the pants belong to can only just get them on as it is.'

Jim saluted. 'Aye, aye. Me and the boys will take it from here!' Then he called down the hatch. 'Oi! Lads! Another load . . . and keep an eye on the big pants!'

Suddenly ten more rats jumped out of the hatch, and manoeuvred the basket full of washing down through the hole. The hatch door closed.

'Have you seen the captain?' Tom asked Jim.

'Yes. He is in his cabin sorting out the lists and invoices. Follow me!' Jim turned and walked aft towards another hatch. The others followed.

There were some steps inside the hatch, and as they made their way down them Arthur asked Tom a question.

'Who were those birds?'

*Suddenly ten more rats jumped out of the hatch,
and manoeuvred the basket full of washing down through the hole*

'Oh, the crows deal with drying and folding. They are part of the crew. They're very fussy and even fold socks up properly. What happens is that some of us go out into the town and collect the clothes in baskets. As we collect the washing we write it all down on a list so we know who everything belongs to. Then we take it all back to the ship. Jim here then collects the lists, and the rats he works with divide the washing into different colour and fabric loads. That's so we don't get colours running or clothes shrinking. Then the bilge crew put the loads into the bilges and we pump water in from the canal. We add soap powder, and about half a barrel of peppermint toothpaste and then stoke up the beam engine. When the wash is finished, the bilge crew pass the washing up on deck and the crows hang it up to dry. When it's dry, the crows fold it and the rats pack it back in baskets to be delivered back to its owners.'

The party had reached the bottom of the stairs and were making their way along a narrow passageway. Jim pointed to a series of pictures that hung on the walls of the passage.

'These are the portraits of our captains.'

'There are rather a lot of them,' replied Arthur.

'Yes. We elect a new one every Friday,' said Tom. 'We are very democratic. There is a long tradition of pirates . . . er . . . ' Tom stopped mid sentence, looked embarrassed and corrected himself again, ' . . . laundries electing their own captain.'

They reached the end of the passage and Jim knocked on the door.

'Come in!' came a cry. Jim opened the door and there behind a huge desk covered in charts and laundry slips, sat a rat with a huge hat on.

'I've got the latest list for you, captain,' Jim said and handed the list over. 'And these are some visitors that Tom

and Kipper have brought back.'

'Aye! Aye!' said the captain, as he surveyed the group that had entered the cabin. 'Who do we have here? Not a complaint about washing, I hope?'

'No, captain, these good people,' said Tom, pointing at Arthur, Willbury, and Marjorie, 'have had a spot of bother. Some friends of theirs have disappeared.'

'Oh dear! We have got something in common then,' said the captain, sounding concerned.

'We may have indeed,' said Willbury. 'May I introduce myself and my friends here. I am Willbury Nibble, and these are my friends Arthur and Marjorie.'

Match gave a squeak. Willbury had forgotten to introduce the tiny creatures.

'Oh, I am very sorry. And this is Match . . . and er . . . a cabbagehead friend in my top pocket here . . . and there is a tiny fresh-water sea-cow in Marjorie's bucket.'

The captain

'Good to meet you all,' said the captain, doffing his hat.
He looked curiously at the miniature creatures for a
moment, then asked, 'How many friends have you lost?'

'Four. Some boxtrolls and a cabbagehead,' answered
Willbury. 'They disappeared . . . or were rather snatched
some time after Arthur and I went to the market, and to find
my friend Marjorie this morning.'

'How many friends have you lost?'

'How sure are you that they have been snatched?' asked the captain.

'I am very sure. When we got back to the shop where they lived with me, the place was wrecked. It looked as if there had been a struggle,' answered Willbury.

'When our "colleague" Framley disappeared there were no real signs of a struggle. But it was hard to tell, as his corner of the crew's quarters is always such a mess. He was a right lazy critter . . . and unpleasant with it,' replied the captain.

'His corner of the crew's quarters is always such a mess'

'He's about the biggest, ugliest, laziest rat you have ever seen!' added Kipper.

The captain went on, 'It's only his expertise in the sorting of laundry that we really miss!'

Tom, Kipper, and Jim nodded their heads.

'When did you notice that he'd gone?' asked Willbury.

'On Friday nights we always have a meeting. We elect a new captain, and do the profits share.'

'If there is any money,' said Kipper glumly.

'We have been making a few groats, but so far most of our money has gone back into washing powder and toothpaste.

Framley is very, very fond of money and had been making noises about going off, because he wasn't making enough here. That week after the share-out we realized that a few coppers were left over, so we took a roll-call and found Framley was missing. We looked everywhere, but couldn't find him. So we guessed he must have had a better offer.'

'It's only his expertise in the sorting of laundry that we really miss!'

'Tom mentioned that a couple of other rats have gone missing?' said Willbury.

'Yes, it was Levi and Pickles. About a week later they went shopping in the town and never came back. We miss them . . . Pickles is my brother,' the captain said fondly. 'We sent out search parties, but there was no sign of them.'

'Do you have any clues as to who might have got them?' asked Willbury

'This is what I have been investigating. At first I didn't think we had any enemies as we lead such a quiet life, but . . .

There was an incident a few weeks back. We had a visit from a rather odious man by the name of Mr Archibald Snatcher, and a couple of his sidekicks. He said he wanted to welcome us to Ratbridge on behalf of the "New Cheese Guild". The captain that week was a man called Charley. He greeted the visitors and gave them tea and biscuits. Over tea this Snatcher asked if the crew would like to join his guild. Only he was not interested in us rats joining the guild, only the humans! He was really rather unpleasant about rats. Said we couldn't be trusted in the presence of cheese and that we were vermin. Awful he was! So we showed him and his friends a long walk off a short plank . . . and they took a dip in the canal.'

'So we showed him and his friends a long walk off a short plank'

Kipper and the rats all giggled, but stopped when the captain raised a hand.

'There was something else that happened when they first came on board. It was all rather odd considering he had such a low opinion of rats. Framley had been picking on smaller rats and crows all morning, and finally just as Snatcher arrived, a fight broke out between Jim here, and Framley.'

'I was trying to stop Framley bullying some of the clothes sorters. He turned on me,' said a rather distressed Jim. 'He got really nasty and went for my throat. If Kipper here had not pulled him off, I don't know what he would've done.'

'Anyway it all blew over, what with the visit from strangers and things. But Snatcher had been watching Framley fighting, and afterwards said something to him.'

'Do you know what he said?' asked Willbury.

'I asked Framley, and he said that Snatcher offered him a job,' replied the captain.

'It does seem strange,' said Willbury.

'Yes, it does,' said the captain. 'But if he was interested in Framley, how come Levi and Pickles disappeared as well? They were perfectly happy here.'

'What did Snatcher say about this guild of his?' asked Arthur.

'Not very much. Just that it was some sort of mutual organization for the benefit of its members . . . and he kept making jokes about it having "big" plans for Ratbridge,' said the captain. Then he addressed Willbury. 'Now can you tell me a little more about what happened to you this morning?'

Willbury paused to think for a moment. ' . . . We had a visit this morning before we went shopping. But from the sounds of it, it was not from your friend. This was from a slimy man who was trying to sell miniature creatures. He seemed very interested in buying my friends, but I sent him packing. Said his name was Gristle.'

'It was me what was serving them tea.'

'Gristle!' said Jim. 'I think that that was the name of one of Snatcher's sidekicks!'

'Are you sure?' asked Arthur.

'It was me what was serving them tea. I am sure he called one of them Gristle when he was asking him to pass the sugar,' replied Jim.

'Then I think all the disappearances are linked,' said Willbury. 'What did this Snatcher look like?'

'Big bloke with sideburns . . . and a glass eye,' replied Jim.

Arthur looked at Willbury. 'It's him! The leader of the hunt . . . '

'Yes,' replied Willbury. 'I think we know who has got your wings . . . and our friends!'

An air of unease filled the cabin.

'Where does this Snatcher hang out?' Willbury asked the captain.

'That's what I have been investigating! There is a building called the Cheese Hall that Snatcher mentioned. He said he wanted to restore it to its former glory.'

'Yes, I know it,' said Willbury. 'But it has been deserted for years!'

'I was there last night on the roof,' said Arthur. 'I thought I heard something inside!'

Everybody turned to look at Arthur. Then the captain spoke again.

'Interesting. I had someone go down and have a look at that place. I'll get him to come and tell you everything he told me.' The captain turned to Jim. 'Do you think you could go and find Bert?'

Jim disappeared out of the door to the cabin.

'Have you contacted the police?' Willbury said.

There was a silence in the cabin, while the crew of the nautical laundry looked awkward.

Willbury addressed the captain. 'I see. Does this have something to do with your beam engine?'

'Er . . . Yes . . . and a few other things. We have a strange relationship with the police,' the captain replied, while trying to avoid Willbury's gaze.

There was a noise from the corridor, and the captain looked relieved. Jim had returned with Bert.

'Ah! Bert,' the captain said. 'Would you like to fill my new friends in on what you told me about the Cheese Hall?'

'Certainly, Guv!' Bert lifted a beret he was wearing and pulled a small notebook out from under it. 'Three weeks ago tonight—the second of September at nine thirty-three p.m.

—I approached the Cheese Hall from the southern side, after instruction to do same. I was wearing a green vest and had eaten three . . . '

*Bert lifted a beret he was wearing and
pulled a small notebook out from under it*

The captain stopped him. 'Bert! Get to the point!'

'All right then!' Bert looked rather disappointed. 'Something is going on in there! The place is boarded up and is supposed to be up for sale . . . but I saw lights, and heard Things!'

'What things?' asked Willbury.

'Strange, bleating, moaning things!' Bert replied dramatically.

'I heard something like that when I was there,' said Arthur. 'I thought it could have been cheeses.'

'Did you manage to have a look inside?' asked Willbury.

'No.' Bert sounded rather sorry that he couldn't help. 'There was no way I could get in as the place is built like the Bank of England. It's mouse and rat proof . . . I asked the local mice. Guess a Cheese Guild would want to keep their cheese safe!'

'Did you try knocking on the front door?' asked Willbury.

'All right then!' Bert looked rather disappointed.

Bert looked rather embarrassed. 'I didn't think of that.'

'I find the direct approach often works. It might be well worth a go, and we have little to lose,' said Willbury.

'We should storm the place!' said Kipper.

Willbury looked a little shocked. 'We might find ourselves in even worse trouble if we do go down that route . . .'

'So when do you think we should go?' asked Tom.

'Can't we go now?' said Arthur. 'We have got no idea what they might be doing to our friends.'

'I agree,' said Willbury. 'But if they are up to no good in the Cheese Hall it might be as well not to raise their suspicions. I think I should go alone and see what I can find out.'

'I don't like that idea,' said the captain. 'Anything could happen to you. If you go to the door, the rest of us can hide out of sight, but we should be at hand, just in case there is any trouble.'

'How about we hide in the Nag's Head Inn, opposite the Cheese Hall? We can watch through the windows,' said Tom.

'I think we should get the whole crew together for this,' said Kipper.

'Well, what are we going to do then?' asked Arthur.

'OK, well, I suggest that Mr Nibble waits here for ten minutes to allow the rest of us to get to the Nag's Head, then he comes down and tries knocking on the front door of the Cheese Hall. We'll watch from the pub.'

Willbury turned to his friends. 'Marjorie, I'm so sorry you've got caught up in this. I promise we'll try to solve your problem as soon as we find our friends. Why don't you and Arthur stay here and look after the tiny creatures while the rest of us go to the Cheese Hall?'

Marjorie shook her head. 'I'd like to come. I might be able to be useful and I—well, I'd like to help if I can.'

'I'm coming too,' said Arthur in a determined voice. 'Fish and Egg and Shoe and Titus are my friends.'

'Very well,' said Willbury reluctantly. 'But I do think it best if we leave Match, the cabbagehead, and the poor sea-cow here on the ship. They could easily get hurt if there was any trouble.' He turned to the captain. 'Do you have somewhere they could safely stay?'

The captain thought for a moment. 'We have a rather plush box that used to house the sextant before Kipper dropped it over the side. The boxtroll and the cabbagehead could use that.'

Kipper was going red, and looked as if he was about to cry.

'Don't worry, Kipper. Nobody knew how to use it

anyway.' The captain got down off his chair and pulled a pile of papers off a mahogany box on the floor. Then he opened it. It was lined with deep red padded velvet.

Kipper dropped it over the side

'It's a bit too small for a rat to sleep in but I am sure it would suit your friends here. Will the sea-cow be all right stopping in her bucket for the moment?'

'I think so. Maybe we could find something larger for her later,' said Willbury. He lifted the tiny cabbagehead out of his pocket from where it had been watching the proceedings and placed it gently in the padded box. It immediately lay down and closed its eyes. Then Arthur leant down and allowed the boxtroll to join the cabbagehead. Match looked round the box and noticed a number of small spare parts fixed to the inside of the lid. He smiled, put his nut and bolt in one corner of the box, then set about quickly removing all the spare parts and piling them up with his nut and bolt. Then he cuddled up to the pile and closed his eyes.

'Do you think we should leave them anything to eat?' asked Arthur.

'Would ship's biscuits do?' asked the captain. 'They are a bit hard but we could break them up.'

'I think they would do very well, if you have any spare,' replied Willbury.

The captain climbed back on his chair and opened one of the desk drawers. He took out two biscuits and placed them on the desk, then picked up a rock that was acting as a paperweight and gave the biscuits a sharp blow. The biscuits shattered into small pieces and the captain collected them up.

'What should I do now?' he asked.

'I think if you sprinkle some in the bucket and put the rest in a heap in the sextant case, that would do for the moment,' said Willbury.

The captain followed Willbury's instructions, then brushed off his hands.

'Thank you. I am sure they will be very happy now,' said Willbury. 'If you put the bucket down next to the box, Marjorie, I think we can be on our way.'

After a few minutes' organization, the entire crew of the Ratbridge Nautical Laundry, accompanied by Arthur and Marjorie, set off for the pub. As Willbury stood on the deck waiting, rain dripped from the washing above.

*The party of cabbageheads making their
way upwards, to have words with the boxtrolls*

Things were becoming positively soggy!

Chapter 17

CABBAGEHEADS

Meanwhile, far below the streets of Ratbridge, there was much activity too. Over the last week or so the cabbageheads under Ratbridge had been very happy. The water supply had been much better than usual. But now things were becoming positively soggy.

They lived, and gardened, in a vast cavern several hundred feet under the streets of the town, and as it was at the deepest point of the network of tunnels, water collected there. Just in the last few days, too much water had started to gather. The special lowlight cabbages were swimming in water, and it was getting worse.

So a meeting was held, and it was decided that a party would go up and politely ask the boxtrolls to turn off the water for a few days.

Four of the largest workers set off up the tunnels in search of a boxtroll to talk to. As they made their way up through the tunnels it became clear that the boxtrolls had not been doing their job very well. Water was leaking everywhere. The cabbageheads muttered to each other that this was not a bit like the boxtrolls, letting things fall into this state. What could be causing them to neglect their job like this? Perhaps they had acquired some new piece of machinery which they were busy playing with, allowing themselves to be distracted from their duties, the cabbageheads whispered.

When they'd travelled some distance, they climbed up on a dry rock for a rest, and had a cabbage sandwich each. This was their favourite food, and was made of a cabbage leaf sandwiched between two more cabbage leaves.

A cabbage sandwich

As they ate their sandwiches one of them noticed that the rock they were sitting on was covered in netting. Nudging his companion, he pointed to the netting in puzzlement. All the cabbageheads seemed baffled, and twittered nervously to one another.

Then, without any warning, there was a twang, and before they could blink, the net whipped up in the air with them all in it.

They hung in the net for hours, trembling as water dripped down on them. They had no idea what or who could have caused this terrible thing to happen. Then they heard the sound of approaching feet, and it slowly grew lighter as flickering candles appeared. The lights got closer and they could see a group of men, wearing tall hats and carrying sacks over their shoulders.

The cabbageheads in the net

The men lowered the net and dumped the cabbageheads in the sacks.

'These ain't going to be enough.'

'We got a few boxtrolls in the other traps last time!'

'Let's just hope we ain't caught any more trotting badgers!'

'Too right!' And off the party set. Within moments all that was left in the tunnel were a few uneaten cabbage sandwiches lying on the floor.

What Happens Next . . .

The action continues in book 2, *The Man in the Iron Socks*. Arthur and his rat and pirate friends must use all their cunning and courage to save the kidnapped underlings and thwart Snatcher's evil plans. But can they really do it on their own—and if not, who on earth is going to help them? Read the next gripping instalment of *Here Be Monsters!* to discover the answers to all these questions and more . . .

Where have the miniature creatures come from—and how did Madame Froufrou get her hands on them?

Why did the Trouts run off with Marjorie's invention—and why hasn't she told anyone what it is?

What is causing the Underworld to flood—and is there a way to stop it?

W|ho has really taken Shoe, Egg, Fish, and Titus—and why?

Just who are the man in the iron socks,

the Rabbit Women,

and the Squeakers?

Can some tone-deaf crows really help to save the day?

And will Arthur manage to find a way back to Grandfather—before the rhubarb runs out?

Book 2, The Man in the Iron Socks,
available now

ISBN 978-0-19-275541-4

Arthur and his rat and pirate friends are on a
mission—to save the kidnapped underlings and to
thwart
Snatcher's evil plans. But do they dare
venture into the sinister Cheese Hall itself?

And if they do, what—and who—will they
find there?

Book 3, Cheese Galore!, available now

ISBN 978-0-19-275542-1

There is trouble in Ratbridge—both above ground in the town and underground, where the boxtrolls and cabbageheads live. And the awful Snatcher has plans to make the trouble oh so very much worse . . .

Can Arthur and his friends summon up all their cunning and save the day?